"When do you think we're going to hear from Copycat Three?"

"I hate to say it, but I think he'll communicate with me in the same way he did before." He backed up and pulled out of the parking lot.

"You mean, over someone's dead body."

"I'm afraid so."

"And you don't think he's going to kill someone just for the opportunity to taunt you again?"

"We already went through that possibility, didn't we? He's not going to stop, regardless. He already has the urge, and he's going to keep satisfying it until we put an end to his craving. He gave us an opening by leaving that note for me. I'm not going to squander that chance." Jake cranked up the AC, even though the sun had yet to make an appearance. "I thought you were on board with that."

"I am." She rubbed the goose bumps on her arms. "I just can't help thinking about some woman going about her life today for maybe the last time."

THE BAIT

—

CAROL ERICSON

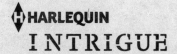
HARLEQUIN
INTRIGUE

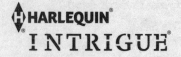

HARLEQUIN®
INTRIGUE®

Recycling programs
for this product may
not exist in your area.

ISBN-13: 978-1-335-40177-9

The Bait

Copyright © 2021 by Carol Ericson

All rights reserved. No part of this book may be used or reproduced in
any manner whatsoever without written permission except in the case of
brief quotations embodied in critical articles and reviews.

This is a work of fiction. Names, characters, places and incidents
are either the product of the author's imagination or are used fictitiously.
Any resemblance to actual persons, living or dead, businesses,
companies, events or locales is entirely coincidental.

This edition published by arrangement with Harlequin Books S.A.

For questions and comments about the quality of this book,
please contact us at CustomerService@Harlequin.com.

Harlequin Enterprises ULC
22 Adelaide St. West, 40th Floor
Toronto, Ontario M5H 4E3, Canada
www.Harlequin.com

Printed in U.S.A.

Carol Ericson is a bestselling, award-winning author of more than forty books. She has an eerie fascination for true-crime stories, a love of film noir and a weakness for reality TV, all of which fuel her imagination to create her own tales of murder, mayhem and mystery. To find out more about Carol and her current projects, please visit her website at www.carolericson.com, "where romance flirts with danger."

Books by Carol Ericson

Harlequin Intrigue

A Kyra and Jake Investigation

The Setup
The Decoy
The Bait

Holding the Line

Evasive Action
Chain of Custody
Unraveling Jane Doe
Buried Secrets

Red, White and Built: Delta Force Deliverance

Enemy Infiltration
Undercover Accomplice
Code Conspiracy

Red, White and Built: Pumped Up

Delta Force Defender
Delta Force Daddy
Delta Force Die Hard

Visit the Author Profile page at Harlequin.com.

CAST OF CHARACTERS

Jake McAllister—This LAPD homicide detective is put to the test when a third copycat picks up where the other two left off, but the killer has a different mission—and it turns personal for Jake. Now he needs Kyra Chase more than ever.

Kyra Chase—Her traumatic past keeps tormenting her as the copycat killers force her to relive her mother's murder, but when the truth about who is behind the copycats is exposed, her greatest fear is realized and she turns to Jake for justice.

Fiona McAllister—Jake's daughter, who lives with her mother, shows up on her father's doorstep, and her secrets not only complicate her father's love life, they put her own life in grave danger.

Roger Quinn—This retired LAPD homicide detective and Kyra's surrogate father makes a shocking discovery that rekindles an old fear he has for the safety of the woman he loves like a daughter.

Sean Hughes—A true crime blogger who's riding a wave of popularity is playing with fire and doesn't realize how badly he'll get burned.

Copycat Three—This serial killer has something to prove, and he does so in a way that has personal consequences for the lead detective on his case.

Prologue

Rule number two. Don't take any undue risks for fame or attention.

He snorted, a little bit of spittle dribbling onto his chin. He swiped it off with the back of his hand. No guts, no glory. Isn't that what Coach always used to say? Or was that no pain, no gain? Whatever.

He slumped in the driver seat, the dome light spilling onto the computer tablet clutched in his hand. His finger trailed down the edge of the display as he greedily consumed the online article about a possible third serial killer copying The Player, a murderer who was active twenty years ago.

The media had dubbed the first copycat, Jordy Lee Cannon, the Copycat Player. They called the second guy, Cyrus Fisher, Copycat 2.0. Now, after the discovery of a body dumped in the foothills of the San Gabriel Mountains, the LAPD feared a third serial killer was at work, using The Player's MO.

The media had better come up with a more badass name than those stupid ones for him.

Squinting at the text once more, he continued scanning the article for information he already knew by heart. After Cannon became a suspect in the slayings of four women, the lead detective on the case, Detective Jake McAllister shot and killed Cannon when he threatened another woman with a knife. Fisher took his own life by ingesting a cyanide tablet when cornered by Detective McAllister with evidence of his guilt in the murders of three women.

He read aloud from the article, his voice booming in the car. "'We identified and stopped the previous two killers, and I'm confident we'll put an end to this one, too,' said McAllister when questioned about this third killer. McAllister had no comment as to why these three killers decided to pick up the mantle of The Player, a serial killer who terrorized women in Los Angeles twenty years ago."

"Confident, are you?" He scrolled down the screen to the picture of McAllister, his large frame in a suit and tie, his square jaw set with determination, his eyes staring at the camera. He hated the bastard on sight.

Drilling his finger into the cop's forehead, he said, "You're not dealing with that idiot coffee dude, Jordy, or that nerd, Cyrus, this time, McAllister."

Raucous laughter erupted from across the parking lot, and he jerked his head up to witness a bunch of drunk frat boys stumbling from the club, the pink neon from the Candy Girls sign highlighting their perfect hair and chiseled features. Probably got tossed out for harassing the dancers—losers.

They couldn't do what he did tonight. He flexed

his fingers and felt the bones of the woman's neck beneath his hands again. It would've been better without gloves. It would've been better with a knife. It would've been better if he could've had sex with her first.

But rules were rules—even though a few of those rules were meant to be broken. Had Coach said that, too? Probably not. Coach had been a stickler for rules.

His gaze tracked to the sign on the outside of the club, flashing different colors of lollipops, and his mouth watered. Maybe he'd reward himself with a lap dance tonight, but only if Barbi was working. He liked her long, straight brown hair—just like Carmela's hair tonight.

When Barbi gave him a lap dance, he could scrunch up his eyes and pretend it was Jenna, just like he pretended Carmela was Jenna and Juliana before her. He'd have to remember to keep his hands to himself though. He'd gotten carried away last time and had put his hands around Barbi's neck.

The bouncer had seen him, or maybe Barbi had pressed her panic button. Either way, the beefy security guy had put a stop to the dance and never even refunded his money. He gave Barbi a tip, anyway, just to say he was sorry, and she'd smiled at him.

He started getting hard thinking about Barbi and Carmella and Juliana and even that bitch Jenna, and he dug the heels of his hands into his temples. He'd have time for that once he'd slipped into the dark confines of Candy Girls.

Taking a deep breath, he reached into his back seat

for the mini cooler, which contained a couple of ice packs. He dragged the cooler onto the passenger seat and flipped it open.

He reached into the console with his fingertips and snatched up the pair of lacy panties he'd taken from Carmela's body. Pressing them to his face, he inhaled her scent. As he dropped the underwear into the cooler, he said, "One souvenir for me."

Then he picked up the plastic bag that contained Carmela's left pinky finger and placed it on top of one of the ice packs. Scowling at the bloody digit, he said, "And one souvenir for him."

Chapter One

Crouching in the dirt, Detective Jake McAllister met his partner's eyes over the dead body of a young woman, a queen of hearts between her lips, her long, brown hair placed over her shoulder, the lower half of her torso naked, her jeans tossed beside her.

With a gloved finger, Jake traced the ring of bruises around her neck. "Maybe he raped this one."

Detective Billy Crouch shook his head. "He didn't rape Juliana French, even though he removed her pants and underwear. No rape, no DNA. He's sticking to the program."

Jake shifted, crunching the leaves beneath his shoes, an uneasy feeling knotting his gut.

Raising his eyebrows, Billy said, "You know it's true, J-Mac. We can't ignore it. The three serial killers—Cannon, Fisher and now this sick SOB are all following some master plan. Our computer forensics uncovered an online link between Cannon and Fisher, and my guess is we'll see the same connection to our current killer."

"I know you're right." Jake sat back on his heels

and lifted the woman's left hand, a bloody gouge in place of her pinky finger. "He's taking their panties as his trophy. They each claimed their own trophy—Cannon stole a piece of jewelry and Fisher snipped a lock of hair—but they all made sure to sever the finger."

"Pulling off their pants and underwear indicates more ambition, greater risk taking."

"I'm counting on that to trip him up." Jake lifted a lock of the woman's silky hair, letting it slide through his fingers. "This one seems to have a type. Juliana had long, dark brown hair, too."

"That's one thing he has in common with The Player when choosing victims. Cannon chose his based on young women coming to the coffeehouse. Fisher stalked women who lived alone and had poor security at their homes. This guy is using appearance to choose his victims, just like The Player did. Only The Player preferred blondes."

"I know he did." Jake swallowed, thinking about Kyra's mother, Jennifer Lake.

"Are you guys finished?" Clive Stewart, their fingerprint tech, held up his black bag and indicated the waiting LAPD crime scene investigators.

"It's all yours." Jake pushed to his feet and said, "Maybe we'll get lucky again like we did with Fisher, and he'll leave a print, Clive."

Clive surveyed the body on its bed of leaves and dirt and nodded. "Could be. He's leaving a messier scene than either of the others."

Jake turned his back on the CSIs as they descended on the young woman. She didn't look like a sex worker, but sometimes you couldn't tell by appearances. Juliana French hadn't been a prostitute. She hadn't lived alone, either. She'd disappeared between a club and her car. There was some speculation on the task force that she'd hopped into a car, thinking it was an app ride.

Peeling off his gloves, Jake strode away from the dump site back to the access road that bordered the trail. Too many cars had driven over the road to be able to make any sense of the tire tracks.

He glanced up at the trees, some leaves crisping at the edges with the coming autumn, others as green as ever with plans to stay that way through the season. LA had its own fall colors that eluded the detection of transplants from the East but made their mark on natives. He could feel and smell the changing of the seasons despite the greenery around him.

As he emerged from the foliage, the gathered press lit up, swinging their cameras and microphones in his direction.

"Detective McAllister, is this the work of another serial killer?"

"Is this the same guy who did Juliana?"

"Another copycat, Detective McAllister?"

He dropped his sunglasses from his head to the bridge of his nose and held up his hand. "No comment for now. Stay tuned for a press conference later in the week."

He ducked into his sedan. Waiting for Billy to join him, he took out his phone and tapped through the pictures he had taken of the crime scene—horrific pictures, indecent pictures. He said through gritted teeth, "What do you do with their panties, freak?"

He jumped when Billy yanked open the car door. "Talking to yourself again, brother, or singing? I saw your lips moving."

"I'm talking to this piece of scum." Jake flashed his phone at Billy.

"Did you tell him we're going to nail him, just like the other two?"

"Something like that." Jake cranked on the engine and pulled around a group of emergency vehicles, including the coroner's van. "What took you so long? You weren't giving an exclusive to your reporter girl-friend, were you?"

"I did go over for a chat, but Megan Wright isn't my girlfriend, and even if she were, she's not getting any details and she knows it."

"Is that why she's not your girlfriend?"

Billy punched Jake's arm. "Are you implying that's the only reason she's going out with me?"

"So, you *are* still going out."

"We're going out, but she's not my girlfriend. I mean, we're not exclusive…unlike you and Kyra."

"Kyra and I…" Jake shrugged. What he and Kyra had was complicated. "Did you finally meet with the PI?"

Billy knew a subject change when he heard it, and he grinned. "Yeah, we met."

"Do you like him? Do you think he's going to be able to help you find your sister?"

"She. The PI is a lady."

"Questions remain the same."

"I like Dina. I think she can help, and yes, she *is* attractive."

"Uh-oh." Jake glanced at Billy. "Is that going to be a problem for you?"

"Moi?" Billy flicked his tie in front of him. "Not at all. She happens to be involved with Jansen, Narcotics. That's how I got her name. The first guy I contacted fell through, and someone in Narcotics heard I was looking. Put me in touch with Jansen, who put me in touch with Dina."

"All joking aside, I hope she can help you find your sister."

"Me, too," Billy said, and stared out the window.

Their drive back to the station was unusually quiet, considering they'd just come from the dump site of a second body that looked like the work of a third copycat serial killer. How unusual was this? The only reason the Feds hadn't moved in yet was due to the success of the LAPD task force in identifying and stopping the first two copycat killers.

When they got back to the task force war room that had been functional for over three months now, Billy took it upon himself to start going through the files of missing women in LA to see if he could find a match to the body in the canyon.

Ever since Billy's sister, Sabrina, had gone missing, Billy had taken a special interest in the lost girls of LA. Jake left him alone with his sad obsession and trooped to Captain Carlos Castillo's office to give him an update.

The captain's door stood open and he wasn't on the phone, but Castillo favored a certain protocol so Jake tapped on the door as he hovered in the hallway.

Castillo glanced up from his computer screen and waved him into the office, his dark eyes flashing. "You don't even have to tell me. I know it's the same MO as Juliana French for our third copycat. I'm tired of this. What makes The Player so special that these sick guys are emulating him?"

Jake dropped into the chair across from Castillo. "I'm hoping our computer forensics team can tell us that. They're still looking into the online connection between Cannon and Fisher, the first two killers. It seems they both favored a certain online message board for crime."

"I'm not going to pretend I understand any of that." Castillo held up his hand as if to ward off too much technical information, not that Jake had any to give him.

"Bottom line—those message boards are a way for people to communicate without sending emails, but they usually require an email address to register. If we have email addresses, we can trace those to IP addresses and locate the person's physical address where the computer resides."

"You lost me at IP address." Castillo ran a hand through his salt-and-pepper hair. "I trust Brandon Nguyen and the others to know what they're doing.

Tracing a link between Cannon and Fisher might help us ID this third killer?"

"It might." Jake rapped on the edge of the desk. "But so will solid detective work. Billy's looking at missing women now. We're running this victim's prints, and the medical examiner is doing a rape kit on the body."

"He didn't rape his first victim. These copycats haven't raped any of their victims." Castillo put his hands together as if in prayer. "They're very careful, aren't they?"

"Just like The Player was, but they always make a mistake."

"The Player didn't."

"I'm convinced he did. The detectives never discovered what it was." Jake set his jaw, feeling disloyal to Quinn, the lead detective on The Player case twenty years ago. Retired now, Quinn still felt the crushing disappointment of letting one get away.

Castillo's face screwed up as if he'd just tasted something sour. "Have you told Quinn that?"

"I don't have to tell him. He knows. He's said it himself. They missed something twenty years ago."

"Whatever they missed is long gone. We had two different cold case units go through the evidence on The Player's five victims, and they didn't have any better luck than Quinn did twenty years ago. Careful man."

"So careful he stopped killing rather than get caught." Jake hunched forward in his chair, ready to launch into his own obsession. "And I'm convinced these present-day murders are going to lead us to identifying The Player."

Resting his chin on the steeple of his fingers, Castillo closed his heavy-lidded eyes. "Are you working with Quinn to prove that?"

"No. I mean, not really. I keep him apprised, I ask him questions, but he's not as convinced as I am that the murderers are linked." Jake paused, studying the dark circles beneath Castillo's eyes. "Is that a problem?"

Castillo's lids flew open as if coming out of a trance. "Of course not. I'm the one who gave you Quinn's contact info, if I recall. I didn't realize you'd get so close to him…and Kyra."

"Is *that* a problem?" Jake's muscles tightened, and his fingers dug into the arm of the leather chair. He didn't know what he'd do if it was a problem. He and Kyra had barely scratched the surface of their relationship, one he sensed could be deeper than any he'd experienced before.

"Not a problem." Castillo waved his hand. "She doesn't report to you directly. She's in a different position than most of the people on the task force. But you've seen some of the difficulties that come along with a workplace romance. Look at Billy and his wife."

"Simone left the force when they had their first kid and still wasn't working at the time of the separation."

"What if Simone wanted to come back?" Castillo spread his hands. "Could be awkward for everyone."

"Yeah, well, divorce is often awkward for everyone." Jake's gaze tripped over Castillo's shoulder to the happy-family pictures on the wall. "You wouldn't know."

Castillo's eyebrows jumped to his hairline, and a pink tinge formed beneath his brown skin. "This is actually my second marriage. The first one ended in divorce—not pretty."

"Never is." Jake smacked a hand on the desk. "We're having a task force meeting this afternoon at four. You're invited."

"Keep up the good work, Jake. You'll nail this guy just like the other two."

"Thanks for the vote of confidence, Captain." Jake exited the office on a phone call, Castillo's tired voice following him down the hallway. The captain either needed a good night's sleep or a look into retirement.

When Jake returned to the task force war room, buzzing with activity, he automatically looked in the corner, and Kyra raised her hand with a grimace on her face.

He took a detour to her desk on the way to his and crouched beside her chair.

"You heard the news, huh? A second killing, just like the first."

"And just like the two killers before him—copying The Player." She jerked her shoulders in a shiver.

Kyra Chase had good reason to dread another Player copycat. Her mother had been one of the original's victims.

"I can hardly believe it, but that's what we've got." Jake touched her knee. "Are you okay?"

"Are you kidding? I'm getting used to it now. It's like Groundhog Day for me. I have to keep reliving these gruesome crimes with every new copycat." She clasped her hands between her knees. "But my feelings right now are nothing compared to the families'. I had a meeting with Juliana French's mother this morning, which broke my heart. She was a single mom and raised Juliana herself—just to have her cruelly ripped away like this."

Kyra's voice broke as her words ended, and Jake did everything in his power to restrain himself from taking her in his arms. Kyra was a professional all the way, and wouldn't want his desire to protect and comfort her to compromise her position on the task force as the victims' rights advocate. Castillo was correct. Things could get awkward.

"I'm sure you did everything in your power to help Juliana's mother cope." Jake cleared his throat and leaned in closer. "We're still on for Quinn's place tonight for dinner?"

"More than ever. Quinn's going to want to know all about this second murder." Kyra's gaze shifted to the side. "Have you heard anything from Brandon and the rest of the computer team about the connection Jordy Cannon and Cyrus Fisher shared online?"

"It has something to do with online message boards. They had the same message boards in their browsing history. Brandon's going to give me a report soon, and when I have a minute to breathe, I'll go through the boards to see if anything clicks."

"Wanna bet the monster who killed Juliana and

the woman found today is on one of those message boards?" The lips he knew from experience to be soft and luscious formed a thin, straight line.

"I know they're all connected. I just have to prove it."

A FEW HOURS later when Jake had wrapped up the task force briefing and logged off his computer, he watched Kyra leave the war room without even a backward glance. They weren't fooling anyone with their coolness toward each other at the station, but they didn't have to feed the gossip mill by leaving together.

He wanted to stop off at his house in the Hollywood Hills first to change, anyway, and Kyra, who lived closer to Quinn, would pick up dinner for them unless Quinn's neighbor had dropped off another meal for him.

Could Quinn help him tie these copycats to the original killer and end up solving the twenty-year-old case? Consulting with the legendary detective couldn't hurt, and getting in the old man's good graces hadn't hurt Jake's chances with Kyra, either.

Detective Roger Quinn had taken a protective interest in the girl left behind by her mother's murder. While Quinn and his wife hadn't been allowed to adopt Kyra, who used to be known as Marilyn Lake, they'd taken a keen interest in her well-being—nurtured her along a horrific path through several foster families, including one where the teenage Kyra had to kill a foster father to protect a younger child in the home, and had sent her to college. Quinn's wife, Charlotte, had passed away a few years ago, but Kyra saw Quinn as the father she never had and checked up on him frequently.

Jake had passed muster with Quinn, which had elevated him in Kyra's estimation, not that he'd faked anything. Detective Roger Quinn had amazing stories to tell and solid advice to give, even though he had that one big failure on his record. Jake had no intention of following *those* footsteps.

After a quick stop at home, Jake reached the Venice Canals, a beachy Southern California replica of the real thing in Italy. The sun had just set, and the spiky palm trees reached into a sky hovering between day and night, awash in a faint orange glow. The glow had faded by the time he crossed the wooden bridge to Quinn's house and knocked on the red door. For a retired LAPD homicide detective, Quinn lived in an unlikely neighborhood, filled with movie industry people, successful artists and a few sports figures. Quinn's wife had bought the house with the proceeds from her best-selling thrillers. Quinn had lost his wife to cancer, but held on to their beach cottage and his memories.

Kyra flung open the door at his knock, the spicy smells of curry wafting behind her. She winked. "I know you like it hot, so I got some extra spicy vindaloo and tikka masala."

With Quinn looking on from the comfort of his favorite chair, Jake touched Kyra's lips with a chaste kiss and murmured, "Oh, you know I like it spicy."

"Stop whispering over there, you two. I'm starving." Quinn banged his cane on the floor for effect. Jake had seen the old man move fast enough without it.

Jake skirted around Kyra as she closed the front door. "Starving for information or food?"

"Both. Kyra didn't want to get into the second murder too much without you—just enough to let me know you have a third copycat on your hands." Quinn eyed him from beneath his bushy gray eyebrows.

"As crazy as it sounds, that's where we are." Jake crossed the room and shook hands with Quinn. "How are you doing, sir?"

"I'd be doing a lot better if these new killers would stop popping up every month to remind me of my biggest failure—and to stop murdering young women, of course. This isn't about me."

Kyra walked past them and squeezed Quinn's shoulder. "We know you care about the victims more than anything, Quinn, but your success is tied to their justice."

He patted her hand, which still rested on his shoulder. "I know you understand, Mimi."

Quinn sometimes slipped into calling Kyra by her childhood nickname, especially now that Jake knew her background.

"We can talk while we eat. I almost have everything ready." Kyra proceeded to the kitchen and Jake followed her.

"I'll set the table." Jake delved into the cupboards

and drawers, grabbing plates and silverware, as Kyra finished opening the cartons of Indian food.

Quinn shuffled to the table, leaning heavily on his cane, and Jake raised his eyebrows at Kyra, who shrugged.

When they got to the table, Jake pulled out Kyra's chair before taking his own seat.

Quinn grunted as he peeled back the foil from the naan and picked up a piece of the flat bread with his gnarled fingers. "Is he always gallant like that, or is he just trying to impress me?"

Kyra choked on her beer. "Both. Jake's a perfect gentleman."

"No cop I know is a perfect anything." Quinn ripped the bread in his hands. "Now, tell me about this second victim."

The gory details of a murder might be strange dinnertime conversation for most social gatherings, but for two homicide detectives and a victims' rights advocate who happened to be a survivor herself, it made sense.

As he helped himself to rice, Jake launched into a description of the crime scene and the victim, and Quinn listened intently, the faded blue eyes in perfect focus.

Jake dropped a dollop of yogurt on his plate. "Long, brown hair just like Juliana's. I think he has a type."

"You also thought that about Copycat 2.0, Fisher, when his first two victims were African American. You were wrong."

"We were. They must've fit his other criteria—living alone, poor security habits." Finding those two young Black women murdered had sent Billy into a tailspin, reminding him of his own missing sister and prompting him to hire a PI to find her.

"I hope we don't find out if that's his type or not." Kyra had perched her fork on the edge of her plate and crossed her arms. "You need to stop him before he kills again."

"I hope we do." Jake rubbed his knuckles on her arm.

He jerked his head at the sound of his work phone, sitting on Quinn's counter. He jumped from the table. "Maybe we ID'd the second victim."

He swept the phone toward him, and his heart bumped against his chest when he saw his ex-wife's name on the display. Tess usually reserved calls to his work cell for urgent matters.

He tapped the phone to answer the call. "What is it, Tess?"

A shaky breath rattled over the line and then she said, "It's Fiona. She's missing."

Chapter Two

When Kyra heard Jake utter the name of his ex-wife, she tried to tune out his words and focus on her argument with Quinn about why he didn't need a second beer. But when Jake's voice rose, her muscles tensed, and she turned in her chair to stare at him.

He was throwing out questions to his ex in a terse, low voice that made the hair on the back of her neck quiver.

She half rose from her chair as Jake wandered toward the front door, out of earshot, but Quinn grabbed her arm and shook his head.

Finally, Jake ended the call during which time neither she nor Quinn had managed another bite of food.

When he returned to the table, the lines on his face seemed etched there permanently, and his green eyes were seared with a mixture of pain and anger.

"My daughter Fiona is missing from her mother's house in Monterey."

Kyra wrenched free from Quinn's grasp and launched herself at Jake. "How long?"

He looked at the phone still cradled in his hand as

if he could find the answers there. Not seeing them, he curled his hand around the phone until his knuckles blanched.

"Sh-she's been missing since around seven thirty this morning when she left for school. She never made it. When Tess came home from work, Fiona wasn't there. Tess texted Fiona, but the text didn't go through—her phone must be turned off."

Quinn piped up from the kitchen table. "Ping the last location."

Some of the color edged back into Jake's face. "The Monterrey PD is working on that."

Quinn pushed back from the table. "Friends? Boyfriends?"

"Boyfriends?" Jake's face took on a greenish hue.

Quinn barked. "How old is she?"

"Fourteen."

"Boyfriends." Quinn shot a look at Kyra.

Jake's nostrils flared, making him look like a horse ready to rear. "Her mother would know about that."

Kyra delivered the bad news. "Or not. I'm sure Tess has already called Fiona's friends. Hopefully, they'll start talking."

"And if they don't talk to Fiona's mother, they'll sure as hell talk to Fiona's father—the hard-nosed LAPD cop." Quinn gestured to Jake's phone. "Start the interrogations."

"You sound like you've done this before." Jake's gaze darted between Quinn and Kyra.

"Once or twice. Get going and take this one with you." He pointed a crooked finger at Kyra. "You need support at a time like this, and if anyone can tell you the thought processes of a rebellious teen, it's Kyra."

Jake took a shaky breath, and Kyra could see the tremble roll through his body. "Do you think that's all it is?"

"You and I both know the chance she's a runaway is greater than the other alternatives. Has her mother checked the hospitals?"

"The police have." Jake turned to grab his holstered gun from the table by the front door, looking ready to use it on whomever he imagined might have his daughter.

Kyra gathered their plates from the table and deposited them in the sink. "Don't leave these overnight, Quinn."

"I know how to clean my own damn house. Go help him out. God knows, he's helped you enough."

Quinn had nailed that truth. Jake had seen her through some rough times, and now it was payback. She planted a kiss on Quinn's wrinkled forehead. "I'll call you later."

As she and Jake stepped outside, he turned to her. "You don't have to come with me. My place is out of your way."

"Quinn's right. You shouldn't be alone right now. Even if I can't help you locate Fiona, you can bounce ideas off me. I'll take my own car and follow you to your house." She nudged him in the back. "Get those numbers of Fiona's friends from Tess and start making your own calls. Quinn's right again. Her girlfriends are going to be more apt to spill the beans to an irate father than to a worried mom."

As Kyra tried to keep up with Jake, rushing home in his muscle car, gunning his engine at every stoplight, she ran through possible scenarios for Fiona. Jake had mentioned to her before that his daughter and her mother had been clashing. This might just be an attention grabber aimed at Mom. Fiona could be holing up at a friend's, maybe even a new friend her mother didn't know. She'd throw her independence in Mom's face.

While squinting at Jake's taillights as he roared onto the freeway, Kyra murmured, "You're going about it the wrong way, girl."

Kyra should know. She'd used every attention getter in the book to usually disastrous results.

Fiona could be with a boy. Kyra grimaced and stomped on the accelerator to keep Jake's car in her sights. If that was Fiona's game, Kyra pitied the poor boy once Jake had him on his radar. Maybe Fiona's mother didn't know this boy, either. Knots twisted in Kyra's gut. There were lots of ways to meet boys these days—many of them bad news.

Kyra kept her eyes on Jake's car as it wended its way up the narrow streets in the Hollywood Hills. Every once in a while, she'd catch sight of the city lights twinkling below. Lit up like a Christmas tree and shimmering in invitation, those didn't look like the mean streets, but you should never let a pretty package fool you. She'd thought Jake was a pretty package, but he'd turned out to be the real deal.

The rumbling of Jake's engine echoed in the canyon as he idled in his driveway. She pulled up behind him and hopped out of her car.

He sat half in and half out of his vehicle, one long, denim-clad leg thrust out of the car, the dome light outlining his profile as he talked on the phone. He ended the call and slammed the car door, making her practically jump out of her heels. The call must not have procured the desired effect.

She twisted her fingers in front of her as Jake scowled at his beautiful view. "Did you learn anything new?"

"Just that my daughter had a social media presence her mother didn't know about."

Kyra's heartbeat rattled her rib cage. "Her friends fess up?"

"Sort of." He clenched his phone in his fist. "Let's go inside. You didn't have to come. I'm not going to be good company."

"That's not why I'm here." She grabbed his hand as he stalked up to his front porch.

He squeezed her hand before unlocking the door and gesturing inside. "Help yourself to something to drink. I have a few more calls to make."

She turned toward the kitchen, and Jake wandered to the massive window that took up one entire wall of the living room. He stared out at those same lights she'd been admiring on the way up the hill, but he probably didn't even see them.

Jake had bought this house from the proceeds of two screenplays he'd sold. It represented his oasis, his escape from the horrors of the job, only now those horrors had followed him home in the most personal way.

He knew as well as she did that most runaways turned up safely, but he'd take small comfort in that when the runaway was his daughter.

She got two glasses of water and brought one out to him just as he was ending a conversation with one of Fiona's friends. Quinn may have suggested Jake put pressure on the girlfriends, but Kyra knew from experience teenage girls could keep secrets like nobody's business. She would've rather traipsed over hot coals than reveal one of the other foster girls' plans to the caseworkers. That would go double for parents, although most of the girls she'd known in the system didn't have parents—at least not functioning ones.

She thrust the glass at Jake, and some of the water lapped over the lip. "Take this and sit down."

His eyebrows shot up as if he'd forgotten her presence. She didn't take it personally.

"Sit and breathe before you blast through that window."

"Thanks." He started for the couch and then jerked to a stop, causing more water to slosh over the rim of the glass. "My laptop. I need my laptop."

Placing both hands on the small of his back, she pushed his solid frame. "Take a seat. I'll get it."

She unzipped the bag he'd dropped in the foyer and pulled out the computer he toted back and forth to work. He couldn't leave it there, as these copycat murders had been occupying his time 24/7…and now he had to worry about his daughter.

Jake had taken her advice, but his ramrod posture and position on the edge of the couch defeated the purpose behind her order.

Sitting beside him, she placed the laptop on the coffee table. "What are you looking up?"

He cleared his throat and took a gulp of water. "One of Fiona's friends admitted that Fiona had a second Instagram page under a different name, a page her mother didn't know about."

"What's the name?" Kyra nudged his arm. "Enter it."

Jake's hands hovered over the keyboard, and then he let out a long breath. "Jazzy Noir."

"Sounds like a…" Kyra pressed her fingers against her lips.

Jake growled as he typed the name in the search field, the whole laptop shivering beneath his furiously pounding fingers. "Like a stripper?"

"Give the kid some credit for creativity, and Fiona didn't invent the secret social media account. Countless teens have been using them for as long as the app's been around." Still Fiona held her breath as Jake found Jazzy Noir and started scrolling through the pictures.

A couple of bikini shots had Jake clenching his jaw, but photos of crazy manicures, selfies with friends, food and even some puppies and kittens had made the cut, too.

Jake slumped. "That's not too bad, is it? I don't know why she'd need a secret account for those."

Kyra's gaze shifted to the side as she drummed her fingers on her knee. She knew a few reasons but hated blowing up Jake's world even more right now.

Whipping his head around, he grabbed her restless fingers. "What? What am I missing?"

"On... On this site, people can also send you messages—messages that don't appear on this page." She jabbed her finger at one of Jazzy's more innocuous pictures of a piece of pizza with everything on it.

Jake's green eyes narrowed, catlike, only more of a jungle cat's than the cute kitties on Jazzy's page. "Private messages from any perv who can see this page?"

"Yeah." As Jake began to click on the screen, she dug her fingernails into his arm. "What are you doing?"

"I'm going to create an account for myself and send her a message." He flexed his fingers. "Brandon Nguyen has been giving me some computer lessons. I'm gonna need them as I delve into the online worlds of copycats one and two. Might as well put them to use to find my own daughter."

"If you do that, you're going to show your hand." Her nails sank deeper into his flesh, making imprints on the tail of his tiger tattoo.

His hands froze. "I shouldn't let on that I know about this account?"

"Exactly."

"Her friend will tell her that she blabbed to me about it."

"Doubt it."

Jake tapped the edge of the computer with the side of his thumb. "I'm not sure how that will help us find her. I believe in full transparency unless that endangers someone."

"Sending Fiona a message on this account is not going to help you find her, either, and when she does turn up, which I'm confident she will, knowing about this account will give you an edge."

"An edge? You make it sound like warfare."

Kyra cocked her head. "Fiona is fourteen, her parents are divorced, her mother is remarried to the man she cheated with and she just ran away from home. What would you call this?"

Jake opened his mouth, but the doorbell interrupted him. He sprang from the couch and stepped over the coffee table in one motion.

Closing her eyes, Kyra clasped her hands together and said a little prayer. Her lids flew open when she heard Jake utter his daughter's name in a tone of joy, relief and anger mingled together.

As father and daughter hugged at the door, Kyra reached over, exited Jazzy Noir's Instagram page and snapped the laptop shut. Then she stood up, collected the glasses and floated to the kitchen.

As Jake marched Fiona into the living room, his arm draped around her shoulders, he said, "You should've just told us you wanted to visit. We would've put you on a plane. Taking a bus all the way from Monterey into LA is not safe."

Kyra exited the kitchen and folded her arms, wedging one shoulder against the wall. Her eyes met Fiona's, which she knew from Fiona's school picture, were the same color as her father's. Any further resemblance to the smiling girl in the school photo ended there. The long, brown hair from the picture now sported bleach-blond ends, the school uniform had been replaced with a pair of ripped jeans, a black lace crop top and black motorcycle boots.

Fiona's eyes flickered, and then she threw her arms around Jake. "I know. I'm sorry, Daddy. I wanted to surprise you. The trip took longer than I expected, and I thought I'd be here before school let out. When we drove from here to Monterey, it took about five hours."

"That's in a car." Jake patted Fiona's back. "The bus always takes longer. Why'd you turn your phone off? You could've called and told me and your mother that you were on your way down."

"I just thought…" Fiona dipped her head and peeked at her father from beneath her long, dark lashes.

"I just thought I'd surprise you…and I didn't want you guys to stop me."

"Stop you?" Jake tugged on the ends of Fiona's ombré hair. "I'm happy to see you, Fiona, but you were coming at Christmas."

"Was I?" Fiona's bottom lip jutted out, and then she glanced at Kyra and sucked it back in. "I know that, but it seemed so far away and I wanted to see you now. Don't send me back. I worked extra baby-sitting shifts for those Newland brat—kids to pay for the bus ticket."

"We'll discuss all the details later. Did you call your mother yet?" Jake checked the phone in his hand.

"I called her as soon as my ride turned into your driveway, Daddy."

Kyra cleared her throat. "Your phone was turned off. We thought your battery was dead."

Fiona tossed her head, flicking her hair over her shoulder in an expert move that must've taken a lot of practice in front of the mirror, and gave Kyra a hard stare. "It *was* dying. I turned it off to save the battery so I could get a ride from the bus station to my dad's."

Jake held up his phone. "How come your mom hasn't called me?"

"I asked her to give me a few minutes to talk to you."

Kyra grabbed her purse. "I'm gonna let you two figure this out."

Jake finally released the hold he had on his daughter. "I'm sorry I didn't introduce you. Kyra, this is my daughter, Fiona. Fiona, this is my…friend, Kyra Chase."

Fiona lifted a hand, waving her fingers with their black-tipped nails. "Hello."

"Nice to meet you, Fiona." Kyra hitched her bag over her shoulder. "Now I really should get going."

"Thanks for all your help, Kyra." Jake took two long strides toward her and then hesitated as he reached her.

He probably felt Fiona's eyes drilling holes into

them, too. He took Kyra's hand, giving it a quick squeeze. "Quinn was right. I needed you here."

As Kyra looked past Jake's shoulder, she spotted Fiona already at the front door, yanking it open. "I'll see you out."

The girl was anxious to get rid of her.

"And I'm going to text your mother to let her know you made it inside the house."

Fiona huffed. "Where else would I go from your driveway to your front door?"

Nodding to Jake, Kyra said, "See you tomorrow."

As Jake bent his head over his phone to text Tess, Kyra walked to the open front door.

Fiona swept it wider for her and held out one slim hand for the grown-up handshake. In a bright, cheery voice, she said, "It was nice meeting you, Ms. Chase."

Kyra moved in and curled her fingers around Fiona's wrist, pulling her closer for an awkward one-armed hug. Then she whispered in the girl's ear, "You don't fool me one bit."

Chapter Three

Jake finished the text exchange with Tess, convincing her to give him some time with Fiona before Tess read their daughter the riot act over the phone. At the sound of the front door slamming, he jerked up his head.

Fiona gave him a big smile. "Ms. Chase seems nice. She's pretty, too."

"She is nice. I'm glad you like her." Jake placed his phone on top of the closed laptop. Kyra had been right about not bringing up the Jazzy business right away.

"You're glad I like her, huh?" Fiona pranced across the room to the kitchen and swung open the fridge door. "Is she your *girlfriend* or something?"

He'd been hoping for more time with Kyra to establish exactly what kind of relationship they had before introducing her to Fiona—that was supposed to be Christmas. Anger and alarm stirred in his gut when he thought about Fiona taking a bus into LA by herself, arriving at night, not telling anyone where she was, turning off her phone. He didn't buy that dying phone story any more than Kyra had.

He shoved a hand through his hair. "She's a good friend, someone I work with."

Fiona slammed down the can of soda she'd taken from the fridge onto the counter. "She's a cop?"

"She's a therapist and victims' rights advocate. She's assigned to my task force." He pointed to the soda fizzing over onto the counter. "Make sure you clean that up."

"I thought you hated shrinks." She lifted the can to her mouth and stared at him over the rim, her eyes so much like his it looked like a mirror image sometimes.

"That's a strong word. Who told you that?"

"Mom. She told me you got in trouble with the department for telling off some shrink who got one of your guys off." She slurped the soda from the top and emerged with a smile that looked too grown-up for her baby face. "Don't worry. Mom doesn't usually bad-mouth you—only when I remind her she's the one who messed things up when she hooked up with Brock."

Jake's heart stopped in his chest, and when it restarted each beat sent a shaft of pain to his head. How had Fiona found out all this information? He had a hard time believing Tess would tell her.

"It—it's true, isn't it?" Fiona's eyes widened in fear. Something in his face must've signaled that she'd gone too far.

He said quietly, "It's complicated, Fiona. Don't assume you know everything from some overheard

conversation or gossip, and don't judge your mother...
ever."

Fiona left the soda and scurried around the corner to throw herself in his arms. "I'm sorry, Daddy.
I don't, really. I just missed you."

He hugged her hard. "I missed you, too. Now, grab
some sheets from the closet upstairs and make up the
bed in your bedroom and go to sleep. I'm going to
call your mother and figure out a plan."

An hour later, when he'd ended the call with Tess
and the water had finally stopped running in the guest
bathroom, he collapsed in his own bed and stared at
the ceiling. He and Tess had figured out an interim
plan for Fiona that would keep her in LA for at least
a few weeks, but Jake had spoken to his ex with a
confidence he didn't feel.

His daughter was not the carefree, happy-go-lucky
child he remembered from their years as an intact
family unit. She'd turned into a full-fledged teenager...and the thought terrified him.

A FEW DAYS after Fiona's surprise arrival, with barely
two minutes to catch his breath, Jake felt a guilty relief walking into the task force war room. He'd spent
hours on the phone with Fiona's mother, her teachers, her LA friends' parents, and even more time gro-
cery shopping and reeling off a set of rules to Fiona's
bored face.

Catching a serial killer seemed easy in compari-
son.

As soon as Jake sat down, Billy scooted his chair

up to Jake's desk and smacked a file folder down, next to his keyboard. "You must've been terrified."

"I was."

"Fiona's going to stay with you awhile?"

"A few weeks, at least. That frou-frou private school she attends in Carmel is going to allow her to do her lessons online. She has a friend here from elementary school she's going to visit, too."

"You're going to have a lot on your plate, brother." Billy held up his hand and ticked off each of his long fingers. "This task force, your daughter...and Kyra."

"Thanks for reminding me." Jake's gaze floated to Kyra's empty desk in the corner. He hadn't seen Kyra at all since Fiona showed up on his doorstep. She'd had an emergency session with a client, and they'd exchanged just a few short texts. He flipped open the file Billy had deposited on his desk. "What's this?"

"It's from Brandon Nguyen. He said you'd be expecting a breakdown of the chat rooms and message boards both Cannon and Fisher frequented." Billy drilled a finger into the page on top. "Let me know if you need any help with this. I can assign a few guys from my video team."

Shuffling the pages of the folder, he asked, "Any luck with cameras in the area?"

"Headlights coming from the body dump site at around midnight, but that's it—headlights. Can't get an angle on the car attached to the lights. It's almost as if he knew about the camera and swerved out of the way to avoid it."

"Something will come up." Jake twisted his head

toward the door of the conference room at the sound of Kyra's voice, and he caught her eye before she sat down at her computer.

When Billy wheeled his chair back to his own desk, next to Jake's, Jake reached for his personal cell and texted Kyra: Lunch?

She replied immediately: Need to decompress?

He'd admit that: Totally.

He even sounded like Fiona now. Snorting, he pocketed his phone and delved into the file Brandon had left him. Their computer forensics team had made the discovery that both Jordy Lee Cannon, the first copycat, and Cyrus Fisher, the second killer visited some of the same chat rooms for a few TV shows and even a true-crime blog.

The two may have communicated that way or shared information. If the task force could trace their conversations, they might find a third party and be able to track him down before he killed again. Jake would put his money on the true-crime blog. They might find a certain sick ironic pleasure in posting on a site where others were trying to solve cases.

He slid the piece of paper on top toward him and ran his finger down the page until he came to the website called Websleuths. Hunching over his computer, he launched a browser and entered the URL for the site.

Inclining his head, he blinked at the rows and rows of links to murder cases, missing persons cases, cold cases. He clicked on a cold case murder in Canada and scrolled through the many messages offering tips and theories and posts with maps and sketches and articles—an entire hive of citizen detectives pouring time and effort into the case of a stranger's murder.

This site must have a thread for the current copycat case. It took him two minutes to find it and already hundreds of posts filled multiple screens. He glanced through a few, and then a breath hitched in his throat when he saw his name in one of the posts—several posts.

Did he want to read those? He didn't need a job performance review from the man on the street. He exited the thread and went to the search field. The computer geeks had given him the names that Cannon and Fisher used for this site, which they'd tracked from their computers' IP addresses. Cannon had used Rusty and Fisher was Rocketman.

Jake searched for Rusty first and sat back in his chair, crossing his arms as row after row of links filled his screen. There had to be a way to search for both Rusty and Rocketman at the same time. The user Rusty hadn't even bothered to comment on any of the copycat killer message threads.

When Billy slammed his hand against his desk, Jake jumped. He'd been lost in the message boards. He glanced at his partner, giving him a thumbs-up while he talked on the phone.

Billy ended the call and said, "We got an ID on the second victim. Her name is Carmella Lopez. Her sister wasn't sure Carmella was missing until she talked to Carmella's boyfriend who said he hadn't talked to her or seen her in days. When Carmella's sister reported finding her car abandoned, a few blocks from the club she'd gone to, with her purse and cell phone still inside, the officer requested a picture of Carmella and recognized her right away as victim number two."

Jake slumped in his chair. Identifying the victims always helped the case, even though it always came with a gut-wrenching sadness. He shot a glance at Kyra, working across the room. He'd let Billy make the announcement to the task force.

After Billy notified the room, he indicated to Jake he'd take care of the processing of Carmella's vehicle and setting up the interviews with her friends and families.

Jake went back to his message boards, the identification of the second victim distracting him. He always compared the victims to his own daughter—and with her here, it hit him even harder.

An hour later, when his phone buzzed in his pocket, Jake backed away from the screen, his eyes blurry and his neck stiff. He could understand how these online sleuths could go down the rabbit hole. He hadn't learned one thing about Rusty and Rocketman yet, but he had some of his own theories about a couple of these cold cases.

He cupped his phone in his hand and read the message from Kyra. He looked up, but she'd already slipped from the war room to hit the ladies' room and meet him at his car in the lot.

He jotted down a few notes in the message board file and stuck it in his desk. By the time he reached Kyra waiting by his car, his brain had lost its fuzziness.

She'd be interested in his progress, but he didn't feel like going through all of it—not even for her. He unlocked the passenger door and opened it, inhaling the sweet fragrance of roses from her hair. This beat burrowing into an internet abyss any day.

They decided on a sandwich place for lunch, and when he gave her a curt answer to her question about his morning, she didn't pursue it.

They settled across from each other at a small window table. Kyra planted her elbows on the table and Jake held his breath. He wanted more than anything to put this morning's research behind him, leave it with the amateurs for a while.

"So, how's domestic life with Fiona?"

It took him a few seconds to comprehend the question, and then he dropped his tense shoulders. "It's been a lot of work the past few days just getting her settled. I actually had to stock the fridge and pantry with some nutritious foods. I worked out an online study plan for her with her teachers and even set up a few social engagements for her. I think it's going to be okay."

"Good to hear." She picked up a menu and held it in front of her face.

"She likes you."

"Really?" She pinned him with a gaze over the top of the menu, her blue eyes narrowed to slits.

"She said—" he held up one finger "—Ms. Chase seems nice and she's pretty."

"You got *like* out of that?"

He shook open his own menu. "It's better than I

hoped for. Fiona's never met anyone I've dated before."

"She's a risk taker, isn't she? Bought a bus ticket from Monterey to LA, arrived at a bus depot in downtown LA in the middle of the night and called up a car to your place in the Hollywood Hills. A lot of girls her age wouldn't have the…guts to make that trip alone."

"When I think of her riding on that bus by herself and arriving downtown…" Jake clenched his teeth and an actual shiver ran down his spine. "It scares the hell out of me."

"Yeah, she reminds me of me." She held up a hand. "And before you get all googly-eyed about that idea, let me refresh your very recent memory. I was a horrible teenager."

"You think Fiona's horrible?" Jake's mouth twisted into a smile.

"I don't know her well enough, yet." Kyra laughed. "I'm just giving you a heads-up."

Kyra must've sensed he was on overload because she didn't bring up the copycat case at all through lunch. Her mood lightened his, and he attributed her positive outlook to the fact that her stalker hadn't resurfaced with this third killer.

Someone who was familiar with Kyra's past as the daughter of one of The Player's victims had decided to torment her with that fact during the first two copycat killing sprees. She hadn't heard one word from him since they'd found the second killer, and that killer had taken his own life.

As the waiter cleared away their plates, Kyra said,

"I told Quinn about your daughter. He was relieved and impressed in a weird way that she made her way from Monterey to your doorstep all by herself."

"Thanks for letting him know." He toyed with Kyra's fingers. "I think my situation reminded him of his days with you."

"Yeah, I'm not the only one who saw an echo of my behavior in Fiona's. Quinn muttered something on the phone about how you were going to have your hands full." She squeezed his hand. "But we'll be more than happy to help you out."

"Thanks, I think." Jake reluctantly disentangled his fingers from Kyra's as his work phone rang. "McAllister."

Billy's clipped tones assaulted his ear. "Another body. I'm already in the field. I'll meet you there."

Jake scribbled the address on a napkin and met Kyra's gaze as he ended the call. "Another victim. Hikers found the body near Tujunga Canyon."

"I'm coming with you." She waved her hand at the waiter for the check.

"I can't let you into the crime scene."

"Got it." She raised two fingers, Boy Scout fashion. "I'll keep my distance, Detective."

On the way to the location of the latest victim, Kyra made up for lost time over lunch by querying him about his search of the message boards.

"I confess." He released the steering wheel and held up both hands. "I got lost in the weeds for a cold case on Websleuths, a true crime discussion board, and wasted a lot of time."

"I'm assuming you checked the discussion threads for the copycat killers."

"I did a search on their usernames, which Brandon gave me, and neither of them ever commented on their own cases. Probably didn't want to seem too knowledgeable."

"That's just creepy." She rubbed her arms. "I dipped into a few of those message boards on The Player, but I had to bounce. I couldn't take it. Some of those posters knew as much about the case as I did. I always wondered if The Player was there, following along…laughing."

"Probably not a good pursuit for you, and neither is this." He pulled behind a few emergency vehicles and spotted Billy's car. The medical examiner wouldn't be here for a while.

He twisted his head in her direction. "Wait here."

"I'm not going to sit in the car." She pointed out the window. "I see my friend Megan with her cameraperson. I'll go talk to her."

Jake slid out of the car, grabbing his jacket on the way. He punched his arms into the sleeves as he trudged toward the trailhead. This third killer had copied the method of the first copycat, who had murdered his victims elsewhere and dumped their bodies in the vast canyons that ringed the LA basin. The second copycat had killed his victims in their homes and left them there. The Player had been known to do both, experimenting with the best method.

He approached the yellow tape marking the boundaries of the crime scene, and Billy met him at the edge, pinching a white envelope between his gloved fingers, creases of worry across his forehead.

Jake's heart did a backflip in his chest. "What is it? Is this not our guy?"

"Oh, it's our guy, all right—severed finger, queen of spades between the victim's lips, underwear missing—but he added something this time." Billy held out the envelope. "It's addressed to you…personally."

Jake's mouth went dry. He struggled into a pair of gloves and took the unsealed envelope from Billy. He lifted the flap and carefully pulled out a single sheet of paper, cut to fit the size of the envelope.

The corner of his eye twitched as he scanned the block printing with blue ballpoint pen.

Billy crowded him. "What's it say?"

He turned the note toward Billy and said, "'Game on.'"

Chapter Four

Kyra narrowed her eyes as both Jake and Billy emerged from the crime scene, their faces alight with some inner excitement, or maybe their gaits signaled the elation—springy, jaunty almost.

Kyra nudged Megan, her friend and a reporter for KTOP. "There's my ride. Talk to you later."

"Anything you can give me…friend." Megan held her hand to her ear, mimicking a telephone. "God knows, Billy won't tell me a thing."

With her heart fluttering, Kyra slid into the passenger seat of Jake's sedan before he reached it. They'd found something this time.

He joined her in the car and sat, clenching the steering wheel for a few seconds before cranking the engine. "He left something for me."

Kyra choked at the unexpected words. "For you, personally?"

"He left a note in an envelope with my name on it."

A feather of fear brushed the back of her neck, but she shrugged it off. Unless he lived under a rock, of course the killer would know the identity of the lead detective on his case.

Smoothing her hands against her slacks, she said, "That's good, isn't it?"

"More opportunity for clues. More room for error. I can't imagine Jordy Lee Cannon or Cyrus Fisher risking a note, can you?"

"Definitely not Fisher, way too careful. Cannon didn't have enough bravado to do that." She drummed her fingers on her knee. "This guy's a different animal."

"Emphasis on animal. He murdered a young woman—strangled her, dumped her body." Jake pulled away from his parking space a little too quickly, and the car lurched, spitting sand and gravel out behind it.

"Can you tell me what the note said?"

"I can tell you if you keep the contents to yourself."

She nodded. "Goes without saying. You already know how good I am at keeping secrets."

One side of his mouth lifted. "The note said, 'Game on.'"

"Oh, that's original." She rolled her eyes. "Not exactly a Ted Kaczynski style of manifesto that's worth releasing to the public, is it?"

"Nope."

A muscle throbbed at the corner of Jake's mouth, showing her he had more on his mind. He'd tell her when he deemed it necessary.

She asked, "Do you have the note with you?"

"Left it with the other evidence so Clive can check for prints and the lab can look for DNA transfer cells."

"Are you going to respond?" She held her breath, watching a gamut of emotions play across Jake's face.

"I'll discuss my options with Captain Castillo, but I think I almost have to. Communication with the killer can lead to more evidence, slipups on his part." He rubbed his chin. "The Player never communicated with Quinn, did he?"

"Never. Didn't communicate with the press, either. But, so far, these copycats haven't been as particular as The Player."

"They're in his fan club, though."

Kyra clutched her seat belt with one hand as Jake took the next corner too fast. "What do you mean by that?"

"We know Cannon and Fisher are connected somehow through this true crime message board. Maybe there are a bunch of them who admire The Player. The posters to the board can hold private chats away from the main message board. They're probably communicating that way to exchange their sick ideas and gush over The Player."

"They all stamp their own personality or particular fetish onto the murder—jewelry, lock of hair, underwear. They all strangle to avoid blood evidence. Two dump the bodies to mask the crime scene. One killed in the victims' homes to avoid being in public." She'd been ticking off the killers' similarities and differences on her fingers and as she held up another digit, Jake interrupted her.

"They leave a playing card and sever a pinkie finger to pay homage to The Player."

"And you haven't brought one of them in alive, yet." She drilled a finger into the dashboard. "That's unusual. Usually these guys want the accolades and attention."

"The Player never did."

"The Player had a strong sense of self-preservation." Kyra reached for her seat belt as Jake cruised into the parking lot of the Northeast Division.

"This current guy is veering way outside the playbook there. He wants his glory, and he's determined to use me to get it."

Kyra's gaze flicked over Jake's profile, which looked carved from stone. "You're going to let him?"

"He can use me all he wants until his hubris trips him up…and I'll be right there to catch him."

KYRA SPENT THE rest of the afternoon compiling a list of the most recent victim's friends and family members. The task force had already ID'd her as Maggie Harkenridge, wedding planner who disappeared after a night on the town. She matched the physical description of the previous two victims, with her long, brown hair. This guy had a type.

After Kyra left the station, she ran her rape survivors group, and then sent Jake a quick text before heading home to change for dinner with a friend. A week ago, she'd penciled in this night for Jake, but that was before Fiona showed up on his doorstep.

She thought Jake might suggest pizza and a movie

at his place so she and Fiona could get to know each other a little, but maybe Jake could read his daughter better than Kyra thought he could. Despite her smiles and happy banter, Fiona had not been happy to see a woman at Dad's house. She'd also been lying through her teeth about the dying phone and thinking the bus would reach LA before school let out.

She got it, all of it, but Jake and Tess had better stop letting Fiona call the shots or they'd wind up in a world of hurt. They could consult with Quinn on that.

As she locked up her office, Jake texted her back. He and Fiona *were* ordering pizza in—just not with her. He promised her a next time and she sent him a text back with thumbs-up and kissy-face emojis. The man had a lot to juggle right now.

Kyra spent the evening with her friend Mel, a relatively new mom, who had been anxious having her first night away from her five-month-old baby. So anxious, she'd spent half the time with Kyra Face-Timing her husband to make sure he was doing everything according to plan.

Kyra didn't mind and enjoyed Mel's stories about and pictures of the baby. Seemed everyone wanted to be with their children tonight.

When she got back to her apartment in Santa Monica, Kyra dumped her leftover chicken into a bowl outside for Spot, the stray cat she fed, and made a cup of green tea. Setting the mug on the coffee table, Kyra curled one leg beneath her on the couch. She pulled her laptop onto her thighs and logged in to her computer. Her emails held no promise of anything interesting so she launched a browser, hoping to get in a little late-night shopping.

Her fingers hovered over the keyboard, but instead of bringing up her favorite online shoe store, she did a search for Websleuths, the true crime discussion board. She clicked on the link, and threads for missing people, murder victims and ongoing investigations filled the screen.

The website boasted three different discussion boards for the three distinct copycat killers. Discussion on the first two killers had waned, but the thread on the current killer buzzed with activity.

She scrolled through the theories, links to other articles, maps of the dump sites and memorials to the three victims. Some of the members already had details about the three victims that Kyra didn't even know yet.

The posters knew about the task force and called out Jake and Billy by name in several messages. They even knew the detectives' nicknames—J-Mac and Cool Breeze. Jake and Billy had also caused some hearts to flutter among the amateur sleuths.

Kyra's mouth quirked into a smile as she slurped her tea. She could understand that, but how did they get all this information?

She clicked away from The Player copycat boards and perused some of the other active cases. She spotted the cold case in Canada of the murdered Realtor Jake had mentioned. Apparently, DNA existed from that case, and the posters were clamoring for a genetic investigation similar to the one that had caught the Golden State Killer. If only The Player had left behind DNA. The bastard had been too careful for that, and his minions were following suit.

She stared at the usernames populating the screen—Jersey Girl, Lil Mama, Sherlock, Poppy, Mass Guy, Online Dick—Jordy Cannon and Cyrus Fisher had been posting on these boards. Did they also have innocuous usernames indicating their location or their interest in sleuthing? Although the task force knew the names, Jake hadn't revealed them to her. She'd been surprised he'd let slip the name of this message board.

Was the current copycat on here now? Was this how they all met? Had they exchanged knowledge and tips in private chats? Jake said neither Cannon nor Fisher had posted on the copycat killer threads, but they had to have been posting on other current crimes that saw a lot of action or their posts would've stood out in the wilderness if they'd been commenting on cold cases.

Kyra rolled down the page, keeping her eye on the number of posts for each board and the most recent messages to that board. A discussion on a missing college girl in Alabama showed promise.

Ugh, that sounded bad even for her.

Kyra clicked on the link to create an account with Websleuths. Staring at the blinking cursor in the username field, she reached for her tea. She should choose a name to indicate that she resided in Southern California. She started entering a name and then deleted it. She had to be a man. Her fingers tapped the keyboard, and then she backed out of that name.

She cradled her mug and studied the contents as she swirled her tea. She made a decision—one that had been swirling at the edge of her consciousness, just like this tea.

She clunked her mug back on the table, missing the coaster by a mile, and entered the only name that made sense: *Laprey*.

A surge of power coursed through her body. She owned it now—the anagram for *player*. Someone had been using it to torment her about her past. For anyone in the know, it would be a clear signal that she had an interest in that old case, in the current copycats.

She finished creating the account but couldn't post right away. The admins had to approve her account. Just like they'd approved the accounts of Cannon and Fisher? Of course, how were they supposed to know who lurked behind a keyboard and username?

Kyra shoved the computer from her lap and padded into the kitchen to make more tea. As she waited for the water to boil in the microwave, her cell phone buzzed against the counter.

She scooped it up when she saw Jake's name on the display. "Hey, you. Pizza'd out?"

"Pizza, slasher movie and I'm done…but it was good."

Jake had squeezed in that second part of the sentence to make sure Kyra didn't think he was complaining about being a dad. He didn't have to prove anything to her, but he did to himself.

"Sounds lovely. Did you happen to tell Fiona you lived slasher movies and didn't need to watch them?" Her microwave dinged and she removed her mug of water, now bubbling.

"Naw, I let her choose. Let her choose the pizza, too, and spent several minutes picking pineapple off my slices." He paused and lowered his voice. "You don't think there's anything…wrong with a girl her age interested in those kinds of movies, do you?"

"If there were, those moviemakers would go out of business. Slasher film makers cater to the blood-thirsty teen market. Why do you think so many of them feature clueless hot teens in cabins or in high school?"

"You got a point." Jake let out a sigh as if that question had been bothering him for hours. "Did you have a good dinner with your friend?"

"Good and a little early. She's a new mom and was anxious to get back to the baby. I guess she doesn't trust her husband to be a good father."

"Maybe she's right."

Kyra ripped open the foil for her tea bag and dredged it in the water. Idiot. Jake didn't need reminders of his own failures as a father, although his wife had cheated on him. He hadn't been the one to let down Fiona.

Jake cleared his throat and took a sip of something. "What did you do with the rest of your evening?"

Her gaze strayed to the laptop on the coffee table. "This and that. Answered a few emails, scheduled some appointments for my clients."

"I just wanted to touch base with you and apologize again for canceling our plans. I do want you and Fiona to get to know each other, but I feel like I need to get to know her first."

"No apology necessary." Especially since she'd just lied to him about how she was spending her evening. He wouldn't be thrilled to find out she'd been trolling Websleuths. "We can always catch up at work and maybe manage a few quickies in our cars."

He choked on his drink as he laughed. "Something to look forward to...and something to fall asleep to."

"Then I'll see you tomorrow." When she placed her phone back on the table, she dunked the tea bag into the water a few more times and carried her mug back to the couch.

She refreshed her email and clicked on the link to verify her new account with Websleuths. She launched the website and scrolled past the different threads. Current crimes made the most sense, and missing women would attract fans of The Player. Her stomach turned at the idea that the man who had murdered her mother and other young women had fans.

She dove into the discussion about the young woman in Alabama, starting at the beginning. The first post in the discussion group contained all the pertinent information about the case, and Kyra soaked in this data to get a handle on things. After reading the messages, she had her own thoughts about the crime. She'd have to take it easy and not come off like a know-it-all. The guys lurking around these boards for kicks would want to keep a low profile.

Taking a deep breath, she flexed her fingers and typed her first post as Laprey. She managed an introduction as a first-time poster, therapy student with a keen interest in this case because of attending the same college where the woman, Amanda Yates, had been abducted.

Kyra sat back and took a sip of tea. Within seconds of her post, she'd earned a few likes. Minutes later, the moderator welcomed her to the board, and a few other members asked her some questions about the campus. She scrambled around online to find some of the answers to the college questions, and she made up answers to others, such as whether or not she had felt safe there. A hundred different girls on any campus could answer that question with their own spin.

She yawned and glanced at the time on her computer. She'd spent a good two hours on the website. It lured you in and trapped you, at least those with the same morbid sensibilities.

As she moved the cursor to the upper-right corner of the screen to log off, an alert next to her username caught her eye. She had a couple of private messages already.

Her pulse fluttered, and she clicked on the first message. She read the standard welcome message to the website, and her breathing returned to normal. Then she clicked on the second message, and her heart skipped a beat.

Some other user, Toby Dog, who hadn't been post-

ing, had sent her a message, and it didn't look standard at all.

Her cursor hovered over the last word, as she read
aloud, "You wanna play?"

Chapter Five

Jake stood outside Fiona's bedroom door and tapped again. "Fiona, are you awake?"

She mumbled and he took it as an invitation, easing open the door. His eyes adjusted to the gloom, and he figured the lump beneath the covers resembled his daughter.

"I have to leave now, but I made breakfast. Don't sleep too late. You have to do all your assignments before you can see Lyric today." He and Fiona had had a good time the night before, and he'd promised her she could go to Lyric's house in Westwood as long as she completed all the lessons her teachers had assigned.

She mumbled again and peeked from the corner of the sheet. "Half hour."

"Okay, I'll be calling you to make sure you're up." He took a breath. Should he tell her he'd be checking up on her and that she had to video chat with him so he could make sure she was really working?

Would that be too draconian? If he'd had a son instead of a daughter, he'd know what to do. A few threats of bodily harm had always worked for him and his brother.

"Close the door, Dad."

He backed up and snapped the door shut. You couldn't threaten a girl physically, but there had to be a way to come down on her. Maybe he needed another talk with Quinn. Kyra had admitted she'd been a handful. Quinn and Charlotte must've done something right because Kyra had turned out…great and her situation had been fraught with more trauma than Fiona's.

As he grabbed his coffee cup, he eyed the bacon and scrambled eggs on the stove top. Had Tess mentioned that Fiona had recently become a vegetarian? Shrugging, he stuffed a strip of bacon in his mouth and left for the station.

When Jake got to work, he sat down immediately with the forensics team that had taken possession of the note from the killer.

Clive, their print guy sat across from Jake at the table and dangled the plastic bag from his fingers before dropping it like it was some poisonous creature. "No prints on the paper, but we didn't expect any. All of these killers have been careful with their prints."

"Except Cyrus. He inadvertently left a partial on that tape. We have to keep hoping they'll make a mistake." Jake prodded the bag, shoving it toward Geoffrey, one of the other forensic team members. "Paper? Ink?"

Geoffrey flipped through his notes. "Nothing special about either. The paper is standard printer paper that can be purchased anywhere from the local corner drugstore to a big box store. Pen is a cheap blue ballpoint, like a million others."

Jake hunched forward and positioned the note in front of Evie, their handwriting expert. "Give me some good news, Evie."

"At least it's handwritten and not made up of cutouts." She pulled her reading glasses from the top of her head and studied the note through the plastic as if looking at it for the first time, even though Jake knew she'd already analyzed every line and swirl. "Distinctive enough that if we had a handwriting sample from a suspect, I could nail him—as long as he wrote in block letters."

"If we only had a suspect." Jake shifted in his chair and took a swallow of his coffee.

"You're going to communicate with him, right?" Evie removed her glasses and twirled them around in her fingers by one tortoiseshell arm. "I mean, did Captain Castillo advise you to respond to him and keep the lines open?"

"I haven't talked to the captain yet, but I'm sure he'll suggest it."

"That won't—" Clive cleared his throat "—encourage this guy? I mean, if he has the ear of the lead detective. Won't that embolden him? Lead to more murders?"

Geoffrey snorted. "You could make the other argument. If J-Mac doesn't respond to him, it might anger him and he'll kill more."

Jake pulled the bag back into his realm and toyed

with the edge of it. "Good point, both of you, but I don't think my response one way or another is going to have an effect on how much he kills. He's got an itch now, and he's gotta scratch it. But making him my pen pal might lead to more evidence for us, might lead to a mistake on his part."

He snapped up the note. "Thanks for your work. I'm sure it won't be long before we have another note to break down, but as long as this one has already been checked in as evidence I'm going to hang onto it for now."

As the forensics team left the small conference room, Jake traced over the letters of the message with his fingertip. The killer followed his own press, knew about the task force, knew the lead detective on the task force. They had to be able to use that to their advantage.

The door behind him opened and he jumped.

Kyra poked her head into the room. "Scare you?"

"Deep in thought." He pinched the corner of the bag and held it up. "Nothing on the note, but if we can keep them coming maybe he'll reveal something."

"He's already revealed a few things." She pulled out the chair Clive had just vacated and sat on the edge, folding her hands in front of her. "He's more of an attention seeker than the other two copycats. Probably means he has a lower sense of self-worth."

"Seems counterintuitive."

"A lot of psychoanalysis is. You'd know that if you were in deep therapy instead of behavior modification anger management." She scooted closer to the table and the scent of roses enveloped him. "Because he feels less worthy, small, he had to make himself into a big man, a bully. You must be very threatening to him."

He blinked and dragged his gaze away from the creamy skin of her throat. He'd once only imagined what that would feel like beneath his lips. Now he knew, and it didn't make it any easier to concentrate on her words when he'd missed her last night.

"Pay attention." She rapped her knuckles on the table in front of him, the slight curve to her full lips a sure sign that she knew what he'd been thinking. She frowned and got serious. "You're large and in charge. Physically, you're a big guy. You're a handsome guy. You have the world by the…throat. You must be very intimidating to copycat three. In fact, that's what you should call him—he'd hate it."

Jake rubbed his chin. "If he only knew I had a rebellious, runaway daughter at home and couldn't get two minutes alone with my woman, he might feel differently."

"He's not going to know that. He sees this—" she framed him with her hands "—perfect image of manhood that he can't hope to compete with, but he's going to show you because he's a killer and you can't catch him."

"Not yet." He grabbed her hand and kissed the inside of her wrist, his lips measuring each throb of her pulse. "I'm sorry about last night."

Her gaze darted to the corner of the ceiling. "No cameras in here?"

"Nope. We could lock the door, and I could ravish you on the conference table."

"You're losing it, J-Mac. I'm pretty sure that thought never occurred to you before. Now, Billy…"

"Are you maligning my partner?" He held up one hand. "I don't wanna hear it."

She slipped her hand from his. "Do you think the pizza and slasher movie helped you bond with Fiona last night?"

"I hope so. She was still sleeping when I left this morning." He checked the time on his phone. "I was supposed to call and remind her to log on to the computer for her lessons."

"One more thing before you do." Kyra tapped two of her fingernails against the table. "I didn't actually come in here to give you a profile of Copycat Three *or* to stalk your impure thoughts."

Jake narrowed his eyes at the nervous vibe emanating from Kyra. This almost sounded like confession time. "Go on."

"D-did you have any luck looking at Websleuths?"

"I only checked yesterday. I plan to dive into it some more today." He steepled his fingers and studied her flushed face over the point. "Why?"

She took a deep breath. "I did a little research myself last night when I came home from dinner. I created an account for myself on Websleuths and hopped onto a thread about that college girl missing in Alabama."

Jake swallowed. This was his fault. He never should've told her which website the previous two killers had been using to post messages, but he did feel a prick of satisfaction. The Kyra from a few months ago never would've told him about her sleuthing. He didn't want to make her regret it, either.

"I'm not sure that's a great idea, but I suppose it can't hurt for you to get an idea of what kind of people post and interact there. It might be helpful to the investigation…as long as you don't actively insert yourself into any offline chats or anything."

Kyra opened her mouth and then snapped it shut. "It's an interesting phenomenon, isn't it? All these amateur detectives. They really seem to care about these cases, these victims. Has the LAPD ever used any of the crime boards for information?"

"I haven't personally, but we've gotten a few tips from the boards. Nothing that ever checked out, as far as I know." He ran the side of his thumb along the edge of the bag with the note glaring at him from inside. "I still need to discuss my response to this note with Castillo. Any ideas?"

"Hmm." She wrinkled her nose as she tilted her head and her blond ponytail slid over her shoulder. "I do think you should call him Copycat Three. I don't think he'd like that at all, and it's good to needle someone like this. It might enrage him enough to make him slip up. Have you decided what medium you're going to use to respond? In the old days, newspapers worked, but not many people read newspapers anymore. In fact, I'm sure this guy has been reading his press online."

"What makes you think that?"

"I'm convinced he knows what you look like. I'm not sure the *Times* has ever printed your picture." She snapped her fingers. "You know that LA crime blogger, Sean Hughes, right?"

"Kind of a loudmouth who gets on the LAPD more than he should?" Jake took a sip of his lukewarm coffee, which did nothing to eliminate the bitter taste in his mouth thinking about Hughes. "Yeah, I know him."

"Him." Kyra drilled her finger into the table. "You should respond through his blog, *LA Confidential*."

"Are you crazy? I hate that guy. He recently outed one of our undercover vice guys, Trevor Jansen."

"I heard about that, but the officer was done with his assignment, anyway. The point is, Sean gets eyes, he gets attention. Anyone in this city who's a crime junkie, including all those people posting on Websleuths, is devouring Sean's blog."

"You think he'd do it? Be a conduit for me?" Jake rubbed his chin. He hated the idea that he'd be working with the enemy, but Kyra had her finger on the right pulse. Sean Hughes got people talking.

"Are you kidding? Sean would jump at the chance to post your reply to this killer. You should definitely suggest it to Castillo."

"All I have to do is tell Castillo it was your idea and he'll rubber-stamp it." Jake swept the baggie from the table and pushed back his chair.

"Really?" She followed his lead and rose from her chair. "Honestly, I don't know him that well, but Quinn does."

"There you have it. Quinn must have something on him to ensure Castillo's support of Quinn's favorite girl." He shot a smile at her just in case she didn't realize he was kidding.

She crossed to his side of the table and punched his arm. "Watch it."

He rubbed his arm, and then he opened the door, gesturing her through. "After you...because I don't trust you behind me."

As Jake walked to Castillo's office, Kyra peeled off and ducked into the task force war room. Jake tapped on the open door, and Castillo waved him in without lifting his eyes from his computer screen.

The captain tapped a few more keys with a flourish and then shoved his laptop to the side, lifting his brows at Jake. "How'd your meeting with Forensics go? Did the killer leave a print on the note or write it with some exotic rare ink?"

"If that had happened, you would've heard about it by now." Jake dropped into one of the chairs on the other side of Castillo's desk. "Still, it is a break, and I think I need to answer him. Everyone thinks that's a good idea."

"Everyone?" Castillo's eyebrows went even higher until they reached his salt-and-pepper hairline.

"Billy... Kyra. She's the psychologist on this team, right?" Jake ran a finger beneath his collar to loosen it. "The more we can get the guy to communicate, the better the odds are that he's going to trip up."

"I agree." Castillo leveled a finger at Jake. "You

just need to watch out. You don't want this killer getting obsessed with you."

Jake chewed on his bottom lip. Kyra had implied that Copycat Three was already halfway to obsession and that's why he'd contacted him.

Lifting his shoulders, Jake said, "If that's what it takes."

"Have you thought about the best way to handle communication? Newspapers don't have the readership they once did. There's no guarantee this guy even picks up a paper."

"Kyra had an idea about that, too. Are you familiar with the *LA Confidential* blog?"

A flush crept beneath Castillo's brown skin. "Sean Hughes? He outed one of our undercover vice officers."

"I know that, but he has the readers we need—the number and the type. If Copycat Three is on the Websleuths site, and we think he is, he probably follows *LA Confidential*."

Castillo smirked. "Copycat Three? Sounds like a Dr. Seuss book. Our boy won't like that at all."

"Exactly." Jake winked. He didn't want to tell Castillo that was Kyra's idea, too. The captain would start wondering who was running the task force. "Can I count on your stamp of approval to reply and do it through *LA Confidential*?"

"I think that's the way to go." Castillo cocked his head and said, "And I think you should consult with Kyra about the response, but you won't have a problem with that now, will you?"

"Aren't you happy about that? She was your hire, after all."

"When we formed this task force and I brought her on, you weren't too happy about it. I think you've come to recognize her...value."

Jake smacked his hand on the desk. "I've come to recognize a lot of things about Kyra Chase. I'll get on the reply once I take care of a few other tasks— one of which is looking through Websleuths. I got caught up in the content yesterday without taking a hard look at the posters."

"Only a few people know that the first two killers were trolling on that website. I want to keep it that way. We can't have everyone and his brother slogging through posts looking for a killer."

As Kyra could do no wrong according to Castillo, should he tell the captain that he'd let that Websleuths info slip to her?

Placing his hand on the phone, Castillo asked, "Anything else?"

"No. I'll be holding the briefing later this afternoon."

As Jake reached the door of Castillo's office, the captain's voice stopped him. "I have every confidence in you and Billy to stop this one, too, J-Mac."

"Did we really stop the other two? Cannon chose suicide by cop and Fisher offed himself with a cyanide tablet. The more I think about it, the stranger that seems to me. Most serial killers give up without a fight. They're almost relieved to get caught. Those two seemed to have…marching orders. Like they're following some kind of playbook."

Castillo shook his head. "The last thing we need is an instruction book for killers."

Jake wandered back to the task force room and stopped at Kyra's desk. "Castillo's onboard for Sean Hughes. Can you set that up, since you know him?"

Her blue eyes flashed. "I've talked to him once or twice. I don't exactly know him personally, but I will absolutely set that up. When do you want me to help you compose a response?"

He leaned in closer. "Fiona is going to visit her friend this afternoon, and she mentioned a sleepover. Would I be a bad father if I approved the sleepover to have a sleepover of my own?"

Her lips curved into a sexy smile. "You would only be a bad father if it's a sleepover you never would've allowed under other circumstances."

"Whew." He swept some imaginary sweat from his brow. "I'll keep you posted."

"You do that. I need to follow up with Carmella's family."

He left Kyra to her work and parked himself in front of his desk and opened his email. He'd barely gotten through the first one when Billy scooted his chair next to his.

"Heard the note was a bust for Forensics."

"It was, but not for other things."

"Damn right. Our boy's thirsty. He wants some attention."

"And we're gonna give it to him. I'm going to use

that crime blog *LA Confidential* to respond to him."
Jake tensed his muscles, waiting for the inevitable
pushback.

Billy stroked his chin. "That Sean Hughes guy,
huh?"

"I know he's not LAPD's biggest fan, but I think
he'll do this for the publicity. It's not like he's on the
side of the bad guys."

"I think it's a good idea. Megan's always talking
about the blog. Her station actually gets story ideas
by reading Hughes."

"Are you and Megan still seeing each other?"

Billy had an on-and-off dating relationship with
Megan Wright, a reporter for a local TV station and
one of Kyra's friends. Jake might believe that Megan's reason for going out with Billy was for information purposes, but Billy didn't need that lure. His
partner had more women at his beck and call than
he could handle—almost. That fact hadn't helped
Billy's marriage.

"Megan's a…friend. Do you need her to put a word
in with Hughes? I think she knows the guy."

"So does Kyra. She's going to handle it. She may
have even met Hughes through Megan." Jake's personal cell phone buzzed and he felt a jolt of guilt. He'd
meant to check on Fiona to make sure she was up and
about, and now it was almost noon.

He snatched up the phone, and Billy wheeled back
to his own desk. "So, you got up."

"Ages ago."

The yawn in Fiona's voice made him suspicious. "Did you get your schoolwork done?"

"Not yet. It's not even lunchtime." Jake heard the clink of dishes in the sink, and he could pretty much guarantee they were the breakfast dishes. "Lyric and her mother want to know if I can spend the night at their house when I go over this afternoon. I asked you before."

"You can't go at all until your schoolwork is done. Remember, it's online, and your teachers sent me a list of your assignments and the link to the portal so I can check that you've turned in everything."

Fiona heaved a sigh. "They'll be done, Dad. Can I sleep over at Lyric's?"

"Text me Lyric's mother's number, so I can check with her."

"Really?" Fiona's voice rose to an outraged squeak at the end, and he pulled the phone away from his ear.

"You know Mrs. Becker."

"It's been years since you were nine years old and playing with Lyric. Get your work done, text me the number, and when I check out everything you can have your sleepover." His gaze shifted to Kyra, hunched over her laptop. Was he giving in too easily?

"Okay, okay. I'll let you know when the work is done so you can check up on me."

Fiona ended the call without a proper goodbye.

Jake placed his personal cell on one side of his laptop and his work phone on the other and launched into Websleuths. IT had given him a history of Cannon's and Fisher's posts to the site and he tracked back through those. They had both been regular posters almost a year ago—mostly writing messages containing theories about missing people or suspects, Cannon occasionally devolving into juvenile black humor.

What had drawn those two together? What had clued them in that they shared the same evil proclivities? After almost an hour perusing their posts, nothing jumped out at Jake. He noticed their posts dwindled to almost none in the past four to five months. They must've been communicating privately by that time, and the police didn't have access to those private messages.

Copycat Three had to be on here somewhere, or maybe he'd already moved his discourse to private messaging. The killers did have one preference in common—they confined their posts to threads on missing or murdered young women. No surprise there.

Jake scrolled through the message boards and favorited a few of those boards. He already knew Cannon and Fisher were killers. He had to find the current one.

He took a peek into a discussion about the missing college student in Alabama. That one would be prime for them. As he scrolled through the post, taking in the usernames, one grabbed him by the throat and his heart slammed against his chest.

Billy plunked a can of soda on Jake's desk. "Figured you might need this to gear up for the briefing."

"Thanks." Jake snapped the tab on the can and took a swig, ignoring the bubbles that tickled his nose while he clicked on a message posted by someone calling himself or herself *Laprey*. "I haven't been working on anything I can bring up in the briefing."

"Still looking at that true crime website, huh? Discover anything?"

Jake eyed the innocuous newbie post by Laprey and bookmarked the page. "Nothing yet. I'd turn it all over to Computer Forensics, except they'd be missing the instincts. You know what I mean?"

"I hear you, brother." Billy took a quick glance over his shoulder and lowered his voice. "Between you and me, those guys are brilliant but they're the first ones who'd get scammed by some lovely lady on an internet dating site. You know what *I* mean?"

"No street smarts. I feel you." Jake clicked off Websleuths and onto his notes for the task force briefing. "Now, you'd better brief me on what you're briefing at the briefing."

BY THE TIME Jake got home from work, Fiona had cleared out, taking her laptop with her. She'd completed her schoolwork, and he'd talked to Mrs. Becker, who assured him she'd be ordering sushi for the girls and they'd be staying in and binge watching some TV show about vampires. Not optimal, but he could live with that.

He showered, changed into jeans and ordered sushi for himself and teriyaki chicken for Kyra. By the time she arrived, he'd poured two glasses of chardonnay and had his laptop open to *LA Confidential*.

As she took the chilled wine from him, she wrinkled her nose at the bags from Mikado's. "You remembered I don't like sushi, right?"

He dug her container of teriyaki from the bag, set it on the counter and flipped it open. "Would I forget something like that? My daughter's having sushi tonight and it gave me a craving, but Mikado's has great teriyaki and I know you like that."

"I do." She touched her glass to his and the wine shimmered in her glass. "Am I allowed to kiss you in here now that Fiona has moved in?"

"Do you think she has me on security cam or something?" He took a sip of wine, and then touched his lips to hers. "I've never really dated anyone with Fiona around, but she'll get used to it. Hell, her mother is remarried and Fiona lives with her stepfather. I'm pretty sure Tess and Brock share a bedroom."

She swirled the golden liquid in her glass. "I don't want to push you, but it would be nice if I got to know her a little on this visit."

"I agree. We'll work something out." He handed her two plates. "I feel guilty about canceling last night's plans, so let's make this more like a date than a work function and eat at the table with glass and silverware, or chopsticks, instead of hunched over the computer with disposable containers and plastic."

"I concur, but you don't need to feel guilty about putting your daughter first."

"But you are a close, close second." He grabbed her and spun her into his arms. He pressed another kiss on her, this one deep and passionate, the kind of kiss that marked her as his own.

She feathered her fingertips across his face and said breathlessly, "If that's second, I'll take it."

As they ate, the conversation turned to the case, and he wondered again if he should bring up that username on Websleuths. Someone by the name of Laprey had been tormenting Kyra about her past. If this was the same person and he was involved in the current murders, Jake wanted to protect Kyra from that knowledge. He also knew Kyra would rather know all the facts—good or bad.

He'd investigate more first and tell her later. Although she was on the task force, he didn't owe her every detail of the case. Some of the officers on the task force didn't know what he and Billy knew.

"Are you thinking about your reply?"

Jake blinked. "What?"

"You're pinching that disgusting piece of sushi between your chopsticks and staring off into space. I thought you might be forming your response to Copycat Three."

He dropped the sushi onto his plate. "You still haven't heard back from Sean Hughes?"

"No, but I didn't tell him why I was calling, either. I probably should've dropped a hint. He would've gotten back to me immediately. He loves scoops and this'll be a big one for him. In the meantime—" she collected dishes from the table "—let's work out what you're going to say to a killer."

"I know what I'd like to say." He lifted her empty wineglass. "Another?"

"That depends." She scooted back her chair, carried the dishes to the sink and glanced over her shoulder with a flirtatious look. "Am I spending the night or not?"

"That's up to you. Fiona's friend doesn't have school tomorrow, so the mom is going to drop them off at the mall. Fiona won't be home until later."

"Pour the wine, baby." Kyra rinsed the dishes and stuck them in the dishwasher while Jake filled her glass and cleared the rest of the table.

She dried her hands and reached for her phone on the counter. She scrunched up her face as she stared at it. "I don't know why Sean's not calling me back. I think I need to set him straight. The sooner you get your word out, the better."

She perched on a stool at the counter and placed the phone in front of her. She tapped the display, and the sound of Sean's ringing phone filled the kitchen.

Sean picked up after the first ring. "Hi, Kyra. I suppose I can't avoid you any longer."

Kyra shot Jake a puzzled look. "Avoid me? Why would you want to avoid me? I have a proposition for you."

"I don't work that way, Kyra. I'm sorry."

Jake lifted his brows, and Kyra shrugged as she answered Sean. "Work what way? You don't even know what I'm offering, yet."

"I'm not going to agree to kill a story in exchange for another one."

"Sean, we need to back up. I don't know what you're talking about. I called you earlier about an opportunity I know will interest you. I don't know anything about some other story."

Sean mumbled something unintelligible and then swore under his breath. "So, you don't know about the story I'm going to post about you on tomorrow's blog?"

"Me? You're posting a story about me?"

Jake had been moving toward Kyra with every one of Sean's words and now stood before her, his eyes on her pale face.

"I thought that's why you were calling, Kyra. I'm going public with your past as the daughter of one of The Player's victims…and the killer of your foster father."

Chapter Six

Kyra almost dropped the phone as the blood in her veins turned to ice water, but she didn't have to hold on to the phone as Jake snatched it from her hand.

Even though the phone was on speaker, Jake yelled into it. "Listen to me, you slimy SOB. If you publish that story about Kyra, I will personally come out there and…"

Kyra put a steadying hand on Jake's arm. He could *not* be making threats against journalists.

Sean choked and sputtered. "Who is this? Is this Detective Jake McAllister?"

Kyra held a finger to her lips. "Where'd you get that information, Sean?"

Sean cleared his throat. "I'm not going to reveal my sources, Kyra. Look, I'm sorry, but I can't pass this up, especially with you on the copycat killers task force and your…uh, relationship with the lead detective on the task force."

An ominous sound emanated from the back of Jake's throat, and Kyra squeezed his arm.

Sean continued his self-justification for exposing

her very private life to the greedy masses. "I mean, it's not really going to hurt you personally. You…um, killed Buck Harmon in self-defense when you were a minor. It won't hurt you professionally. Hell, I think it might bring you more business. Anyway, I—I have to run with it. It's already written and scheduled to post tomorrow morning."

Kyra sighed. "You do what you have to do."

"Now that that's settled." Sean's tone grew crisp. "What is the opportunity you have for me?"

Jake answered him. "There's no way in hell you're getting that now, buddy."

"Actually, once Sean posts the story about me, it makes even more sense for you to work with him."

The tips of Jake's ears turned so red Kyra expected steam to start pouring out of them. "I'm not working with this guy."

"Sean, I'll call you back later."

"I'm intrigued…and I really am sorry, Kyra."

She ended the call before Jake could spew any more vitriol over the phone. Then she grabbed her glass of wine and downed half of it in one gulp.

"Don't you get it? After he posts that story about me and my connection to the case, he'll have even more readers for your response."

"At what price?" Jake placed his hands on her shoulders. "I don't want to see you hurt. You went through a lot of trouble changing your identity and moving away from your traumatic past. He has no right to bring it all crashing down on your head. I can make it stop. I can make *him* stop."

"No, you can't, but I love you for wanting to try." She cupped his strong, fierce jaw with one hand. "Maybe it's for the best. If it had all been out in the open, I never would've lied to you about my past. Once the prurient interest dies down, people will move on to another story."

"There's gonna be talk at the station." He turned his head to kiss her palm. "I don't like the thought of you being the object of…"

"What? Pity? That's not so bad. Curiosity? I can live with that." She pressed a hand against his thudding heart. "If you're by my side, I can get through all of that."

"You can count on it, count on me, and it'll start tomorrow."

"What does that mean?"

"I'm not going to let you walk into the lion's den alone tomorrow. We'll walk into the station together. Anything anyone has to say to you can go through me first."

Smiling, she drummed her fingers against his chest. "You're going to take care of them like you threatened to take care of Sean?"

"That guy." A scowl twisted Jake's features. "I'm not gonna send my reply to Copycat Three through him."

"Yes, you are." She smoothed a hand across Jake's face. "It's perfect. He blogs about me and my past and then he segues into your response to the killer. Copycat Three is going to get what he wants…and so are you."

"Why are you comforting me when it's your life that's about to be blown to bits?" He captured her hand and kissed her fingertips.

"That's just it. The prospect of Sean outing me tomorrow doesn't fill my heart with terror as long as I'm with you. When I'm alone in my cold bed... that's another story."

Jake curled his hands around her waist and pulled her from the stool, securing her against his chest. "Tonight, you're not going to be alone in your bed, and it's certainly not going to be cold."

Once Jake started kissing and touching her, they didn't make it to his bed or even to his bedroom. Much later, sated and languid, Kyra pushed the dark hair from Jake's eyes as he studied her from beneath half-mast lids. "We should move this party to your bedroom."

"Is this still a party?" He ran a fingertip down her spine, making her shiver.

"I'll let you know after I brush my teeth and wash my face." She rolled off the couch and scooped up her discarded clothing. As she faced the wall of glass that looked out over city lights, Kyra clutched her clothes to her chest. "You're sure nobody can see in here?"

Jake joined her at the window, stark naked, and rapped one knuckle on the glass. "You see any houses facing mine?"

"What's that tall building to the right?"

"That's a mixed-use building on Sunset, some offices, some apartments. See how small those windows are? Nobody can see us from there unless they have a telescope trained on us."

Kyra hunched her shoulders as a wisp of unease tickled the back of her neck. "If you say so."

She left Jake to gather up his own clothes and cut through his bedroom to the master bath. She peeked into a basket on the vanity for the few items, including a toothbrush, she'd taken to leaving at his place.

He came up behind her and touched her hip. "I put your stuff in the second drawer."

She opened the drawer he indicated and snatched up her toothbrush.

He swept the hair off the back of her neck and pressed his lips against the nape. "I thought it was a good idea to stash your stuff there while Fiona was here. What do you think?"

She forced a smile to her face and met his eyes in the mirror. "I think that's a good idea."

Jake stuffed his clothes into the wicker hamper and grabbed his own toothbrush. "When are you calling Hughes?"

"Tomorrow morning, but we didn't even start working on your response."

Jake wiggled his eyebrows. "We had more important matters to address."

She bumped his hip with hers to gain access to the sink and rinsed out her mouth. "I suppose Sean is never going to tell me who ratted me out."

"You don't think he did the digging on his own?"

"Why would he? I barely know the guy. Why would he be looking into me?" She splashed water on her face and came up for air. "Nope. Somebody dished on me."

"Do you think it's *him*?"

"Laprey? Who else knows everything? Who else has been trying to make my life miserable for the past several months?" She dropped her toothbrush back into the drawer of shame and spun around. "I guess this is his endgame. I hope so, anyway. Maybe he'll stop after this."

"What more could he want?" Jake kissed her shoulder. "We'll face it together tomorrow."

Kyra left Jake in the bathroom and slid between his crisp sheets. When he joined her in bed, he pulled her back against his chest and draped a heavy arm over her waist. It didn't take long before Jake's breathing deepened.

Kyra lifted his arm from her body and paused as he murmured and shifted onto his back. She scooted to the edge of the bed and glanced over her shoulder at his sleeping form.

Then she grabbed one of his T-shirts, slipped it over her head and padded back into the living room with its fishbowl window on the world. Tucking her laptop beneath her arm, she curled up in one corner of the couch, inhaling Jake's scent, which still clung to the leather.

She flipped open her laptop and accessed the Websleuths site. She clicked on the private message from Toby Dog and responded.

I do wanna play. What do you have in mind?

KYRA HAD BEEN playing coy the night before by not packing an overnight bag with work clothes. Now she regretted it.

Jake had been serious about walking into the station with her, so he'd followed her all the way to her place in Santa Monica and hung out with Spot, the stray cat, while she changed for work.

As she emerged from the bathroom, straightening her skirt, she smirked at Spot circling Jake's ankles. "He's going to get cat hair all over your pants."

"I can live with a little cat hair, but I'll keep him away from you." He cocked his head, and his gaze raked her from head to toe. "You look good. Fierce. Ready to take on the world."

"I'd better be. Have you checked out *LA Confidential*, yet?" She held up her phone. She'd been perusing the blog in the bathroom while drying her hair. "It could be worse."

"I confess. I read it while you were in the shower and Spot was munching his kibble. It's sensational. Hughes's writing style is sensational, but you don't come off looking bad."

She snorted. "I come off like a shady lady from a 1940s film noir."

"Is that bad?" Jake swooped down and grabbed Spot under his belly with one hand as the cat tried to make a beeline for her legs. "That's the way Hughes writes. I can see why the blog is popular."

"Megan Wright already called me, so the media have picked up on the story."

"You talked to Megan?"

"Not yet. She left me a voice mail. I can tell she's kind of hurt that I didn't give her the scoop. She assured me, she would've handled my story with a lot more sensitivity than Sean managed." Kyra raised and dropped her shoulders quickly. "Should've, could've, would've. It's out there now."

"Let's not make this worse by coming in to the station any later." Jake rotated his wrist and stared down Spot's angry gaze. "Time for you to take a hike. I gotta play wingman for the shady lady."

Kyra insisted on taking her own car and followed Jake back to the Northeast Division. On the drive over, she called Megan.

Her friend gushed over the phone. "Are you okay, Kyra? My God, I never would've guessed your background, although you always did seem interested in serial killers in general and The Player, specifically. Did Jake know?"

"Jake knew." Kyra didn't go into the details about how Jake knew, how he'd had to pull every bit of the truth from her by hook or by crook. "Now everybody knows."

"You come off kind of heroic, you know. K-killing Buck Harmon in self-defense while trying to protect a little girl. That's not a bad thing, Kyra." Megan paused. "Any way to track down the girl today?"

Kyra clamped down on the retort that rose to her lips. Megan was a journalist trying to do her job. "I think she deserves her privacy even though I've lost mine. My juvenile records are sealed, so her name won't be public—unless someone outs her like someone outed me."

"Who did out you, Kyra? Who knows your story and would spill it to Sean? Did he tell you his source?"

"I have no clue, and Sean didn't tell me. Would you?"

"I'm afraid I wouldn't, even though we're friends." Megan sucked in a breath. "We're still friends, aren't we?"

"I don't blame you for anything, Megan. Why would I? I don't even fault you for wanting more of the scoop—you're just not going to get it, at least not from me." Kyra drummed her thumbs on the steering wheel. "Unless you don't think you could be friends with someone like me."

"What are you talking about, girlfriend? You're a hero for ridding the world of a scumbag. And your mother's murder? You deserve sympathy and support for that. I suppose that's why you're so good at your job. Can you imagine what your story's going to mean to the family members of the copycat killers' victims? Now they know you can truly understand what they're going through." Megan sniffled. "I'm proud to know you, Kyra. If whoever leaked this story to Sean thought they were going to hurt you, they misjudged the public."

Megan's words made Kyra's nose tingle. She'd been keeping these secrets for so long because the truth made her feel exposed, vulnerable, but maybe she'd been wrong to hide it all.

"Thanks for your support, Megan. I'm pulling into the station right now, so we'll talk later."

When she ended the call, Kyra noticed that she'd received another call and voice mail, from Quinn this time. He must've heard the news.

She knew he wouldn't be happy about the latest development in her life. Quinn and Charlotte had been the ones who'd told her to keep her past to herself. When she wanted to change her name from Marilyn Lake to Kyra Chase, they'd both encouraged her to do so and even helped her establish her new ID. She'd save Quinn's call for later.

She trailed Jake into the station's parking lot and parked her car with the unmarked police vehicles on the edge of the lot. She stayed in her car until she saw Jake's head bobbing above the other black sedans.

Taking a deep breath, she exited her vehicle and wended her way through the cars toward him.

He held out his hand and she took it. Squeezing her fingers, he said, "Ready?"

"As ready as I'll ever be." She disentangled her fingers from his and squared her shoulders. "Quinn left me a voice mail. He must've heard."

"Do you think he'll be upset?"

"I think I'd better see him tonight to reassure him. He never wanted me to reveal that my mother was one of The Player's victims." She tripped over a crack in the pavement and Jake caught her arm. "I don't think he wanted my name and identity revealed."

"Because he thinks The Player is still out there.

But why would The Player be interested in hurting you after all these years?"

Kyra stopped and wiped her palms on her skirt. "Can we not talk about this right now? I'm about to face some curious colleagues."

"I'm sorry. I'm supposed to be supporting you, and I'm making it worse." Jake tapped the side of his head. "Can't turn off the detective."

"I know that." She tugged on the sleeve of his jacket. "Just don't go off on anyone like you did with Sean Hughes last night. People are going to be curious, and that's okay."

He touched his fingers to his forehead in a mock salute. "Got it. You haven't talked to that... I mean, you haven't talked to Hughes yet, have you?"

She clicked her tongue. "No, but we're going to work on your response today and get it to him to publish tomorrow."

Jake opened the door for her, and they walked through the lobby of the station. With her heart pounding, Kyra climbed the stairs to the second floor, which housed the conference room dedicated to the task force, or the war room, as they referred to it. Her knees wobbled, but she resisted hanging on to Jake's arm for support.

She sailed into the war room, her chin held high and her gaze sweeping the space. Was she imagining it, or did the decibel level recede for a split second? A few people looked up and then looked away quickly.

She huffed a sharp breath from her nose and nodded at Jake as she took a seat at her desk in the corner.

Two seconds later, Lieutenant Alicia Fields approached Kyra's desk. Perching on the edge, Alicia said, "Read *LA Confidential* this morning, and just wanted to let you know you rock. I always thought we were lucky to have your expertise on the task force, and that belief has increased tenfold. Keep up the good work."

Kyra blinked back tears. "Thanks, Lieutenant. Means a lot."

As soon as Lieutenant Fields walked away, a female patrol officer scooted a chair up to Kyra's desk. "Hi, Kyra, my name's Loretta, and I just wanted to let you know that I admire you so much after reading that blog. My stepfather was abusive, and he molested me and my sister. It took us a few years to get away from him. I wish we'd had someone like you to stand up for us."

Kyra flattened a hand against her chest. "I'm so sorry you went through that."

After that, a few other officers gave her thumbs-ups, and she started getting emails from some of the family members of the copycats' victims expressing their condolences for her mother and thanking her for her support.

Kyra's heart had filled to bursting when Billy came to her desk and gave her a one-armed hug. "I'm glad we have you on this task force, even though it must be incredibly hard for you to relive these crimes. We're behind you—all of us."

That was it. Kyra squeezed Billy's hand and

launched out of her chair. She stumbled blindly toward the restroom, her throat choked with tears.

When she made it to the bathroom, she crashed into a stall, startling an officer washing her hands. Kyra placed her hands against the metal door, dropped her head between her arms and sobbed.

After a few minutes of release, Kyra tugged some toilet paper from the roll and mopped her face. She hadn't expected any of that. All her fears had been wiped away with a few kind words.

She peeked out of the stall, scanned the empty bathroom and walked to the vanity to inspect the damages. She splashed cold water on her face and dabbed at the streaks of mascara beneath her eyes.

She returned to the war room with greater confidence than when she'd entered it this morning, even with Jake by her side. This time, nobody shot her furtive glances and nobody abruptly stopped talking. Cops were a prosaic bunch, not given to excess sentimentality. That's why she'd always liked working with them.

She clicked through a few more supportive emails from the victims' families and then switched over to the psychological profile of Copycat Three that the FBI had provided the team.

She nodded along as she read, agreeing with the majority of the report. Jake's response needed to challenge the killer's manhood. They needed to unsettle Copycat Three and force his hand.

By the time Kyra had drafted a few responses, Jake texted her, inviting her out to a working lunch.

Forty-five minutes later, they sat across from each other over sandwiches and salads, and she pushed printouts of her responses in front of him.

"This is what I have, so far."

Ignoring the papers, Jake picked up his sandwich. "Do you want to talk about what happened this morning?"

Kyra's nose twitched at the thought of the outpouring of support from her colleagues. "It was pretty awesome. Did you... Did you have anything to do with it? Did you call ahead and read them the riot act?"

"You give me way too much credit or power. What happened in there was spontaneous. You really think anyone in law enforcement is going to hold it against you that you killed someone in self-defense, or that your mother was a victim of The Player? If anything, you solidified yourself as one of us. I just wish it hadn't taken you so long to realize you had nothing to be ashamed about."

"Quinn always encouraged me to hide it, or maybe just to put it in my past." She rushed in to cover any perceived criticism of Quinn. "He wasn't wrong. I did want to put it all behind me. I didn't want to go through college being *that* girl. The freak show."

"Maybe Quinn was right. But you're mature enough to handle the fallout now, and I'm glad it's out in the open. Maybe I owe Sean Hughes an apology."

She tapped the papers on the table. "He's getting your response to a serial killer for his blog. That's enough of an apology."

"Can I eat first?"

"Since I kept you from having breakfast this morning, I'd feel even more guilty if I kept you from lunch."

When Jake emerged from demolishing half his sandwich, he asked, "Have you talked to Quinn yet?"

"No, I listened to his voice mail and he just asked me to call him." She prodded bits of veggies in her salad around her plate. "I think he just wants to make sure I'm okay."

"I think that's all he ever wants for you. I don't fault him for helping you maintain your secrets, if that's what you think."

"I don't think that at all. He had his reasons, and they were right for the time." She gave up on her salad and sucked down some iced tea. "Speaking of good parenting, did you talk to Fiona today?"

"A few times—this morning while she was having a late breakfast and just before I left for lunch as she and Lyric were getting ready to go to the mall. Even though Lyric had the day off from school, Fiona didn't, so I told her she needed to be home before dinner to get her schoolwork done."

"Have you looked any more at the alternate Instagram page?"

"Jazzy?" He dragged a napkin across the lower half of his face. "No, but I think I'd better discuss it with her. I'm learning enough from Brandon the IT guy to make me more and more uncomfortable with that page. It looks like we can't get to the private messages Cannon and Fisher wrote on Websleuths.

They've all been deleted, and we haven't found a way to retrieve them yet. The internet can be a dark and dangerous place."

Kyra's hand shook a little as she set down her tea. Her own private message to Toby Dog's invitation to play had gone unanswered so far. Did she really believe he was some kind of serial killer recruiter?

"Maybe you should confront Fiona about it tonight. Clue her in on the dangers of communicating with strangers online and make her delete the account."

"That'll endear me to her."

"You don't want to be her dear. You want to be her father. I can tell you, there were times I hated Quinn and Charlotte, or I thought I did."

"I know you're right. I'll have my father-daughter talk with Fiona tonight, while you have yours with Quinn. And now—" he shoved aside the basket with the remainder of his sandwich inside and stacked the printouts in front of him "—I need to respond to a killer."

For the next hour, they hunched over the table and crossed out words, rephrased sentences and debated psychology until they agreed on a finished statement for Copycat Three.

"There." Kyra shoved the marked-up papers into her purse. "I'll call Sean this afternoon and ask him to run it tomorrow."

Jake pulled out his wallet and left a couple of bills on the table. "Are you also going to try to convince him to give up his source for your story?"

"I'll give it a try, but I'm sure he won't budge."

Kyra hitched her purse over her shoulder and made for the door.

When they got back to Jake's car, he checked his work phone and then stuck it in the holder on the dash.

Eyeing the display, Kyra asked, "Nothing new, huh?"

"Nobody's confessed, if that's what you mean." He turned on the engine, and his phone rang. He tapped to answer without looking at the display.

With his phone on speaker, the woman's voice flooded the car. "Jake, as long as you're seeing that… killer, I don't want her anywhere near Fiona."

Chapter Seven

Jake scrambled for the phone, dropping it on the console as he jabbed at the speaker button. When he pressed the phone against his ear, he hissed, "You've got some nerve, Tess."

Kyra relegated the rest of the one-sided conversation to background noise as she crashed from the high of the response from her colleagues on the task force to a painful low. She'd always worried her background would taint her, render her not good enough in other people's eyes. Tess had just offered confirmation of that.

Jake ended the call and slammed his phone into the cup holder. "I'm sorry, Kyra. She had no right to say those things."

"But she did have a right." Kyra pinned her hands between her bouncing knees. "Fiona is her daughter."

"Like you would somehow infect Fiona." He swore and swung out of the parking space in the strip mall. "I could've objected to her husband Brock all these years. Cheated on his own wife with Tess, breaking up two marriages and families."

"Brock didn't kill anyone, did he?"

"He wouldn't have the guts to stand up to someone like you did." Jake's jaw set into hard lines, and Kyra loved him for his ardent defense of her—but it didn't change anything.

"Tell her I'll stay away."

His head jerked to the side. "What? No. She doesn't have a right to control my dating life."

Kyra put her hand on Jake's corded forearm, the tail of his tiger tattoo exposed by his rolled-up sleeves, almost pulsing. "Just for now. Just while Fiona's with you. We can still see each other at work, and we'll figure it out when Fiona leaves. Maybe Tess will have calmed down by then."

"I have no idea how she found out. She doesn't even practice criminal law, so I don't think she'd be trolling the internet for blogs like *LA Confidential*."

"Fiona told her."

Shifting in his seat, Jake flipped up the AC. "Why would she do that?"

Kyra swallowed. She hadn't meant to blurt out those words. "Maybe the news about me scared her."

She doubted much of anything scared Fiona, but Kyra shouldn't have shown her hand that first night. She should've pretended that Fiona was pulling the wool over her eyes as much as she was over her father's.

Jake said, "I'll talk with her."

"Not about me." She squeezed Jake's solid thigh. "Don't try to talk her out of anything. She'll only dig in."

Jake grunted. "You're the therapist."

When they got back to the station, they went their separate ways and Kyra contacted Sean Hughes to talk to him about Jake's response to Copycat Three.

Sean's excitement for the story squelched any residual awkwardness over the blog he'd posted about her. After she emailed Sean the copy of Jake's communication, Kyra sat back in her seat and lowered her voice, cupping the phone against her face.

"I suppose you're not going to tell me where you learned about my past, are you?"

"Sources and all that, Kyra. I can't. I'd lose all credibility. Not even Megan, your friend, would reveal that to you."

"I know." She tapped a pen on the edge of her laptop. "Just be careful."

"Careful?"

"I've had some strange communications with someone who knows all about me. This same person seems to be connected to the current copycat slayings. If he's the same person who clued you in to my history, I'm telling you he's unstable. He may have even been responsible for the death of a homeless woman he used to reach me. When he was done with her, she died in a hit-and-run accident."

Sean caught his breath over the phone. "You have proof of this?"

"I do not. I have only my suspicions, but he's not someone you want too close to you."

"Probably not someone I want to cross, either."

She pounced on his words. "So, you're saying it's the same person?"

Sean clicked his tongue. "I'm not saying anything like that. Truth be told, my source is anonymous, but I was able to back up everything he…or she told me. That's all I'm saying."

"If you feel he or she has pertinent information about these current crimes, that's a different matter. Lives are in peril. You have a duty to come clean— just like if one of my clients threatened to do harm. I could step away from patient confidentiality and report that."

"I understand my duty, Kyra. It's nothing like that." He coughed. "How have the revelations gone for you today? I hope you've seen the comments on the blog. Most people are applauding you for taking out a dirtbag and lauding you for helping families of other murder victims. You're coming through this smelling like a rose."

"It's been fine. No hard feelings." Except it probably ruined any chance of a relationship with the man she loved.

"Good to hear it. I'm not completely heartless."

"Just run the response tomorrow and work with the police for a change."

"I'm always willing to work with the police…as long as they stay in their lane."

Kyra glanced up at Clive, standing at her desk and raising his eyebrows to his bald pate.

Smiling, she held up one finger to him. "Gotta

go, Sean. This time I'm looking forward to the blog tomorrow."

Once she'd hung up, Clive said, "Hope I didn't interrupt you. Was that the *LA Confidential* blogger?"

"It was. I heard you didn't find any prints on the note."

"No luck this time." Clive shuffled his feet. "I wasn't here when you came in this morning, so I just wanted to add my support to all the rest you've been getting from the team."

"Thanks, Clive. That means a lot."

The warm glow in her belly stayed with her the rest of the afternoon, but all the support in the world wouldn't compensate for losing Jake. His daughter had to come first.

Before she wrapped up, she made the call she'd been dreading.

Quinn answered on the first ring. "Took you a while to get back to me. I would've been worried, but I knew you'd be at the station and have Jake to look after you."

"I can look after myself, Quinn." She might have to if Jake's ex forced him out of her life. "But I'm fine. Everyone at the station has been great."

"I didn't doubt that, but...do you have plans tonight?"

"I think I do now."

"Rose sent over some stew, and I can't hope to eat it all myself. You can come over anytime."

"I have a group after I leave the station, but when that's over I'm all yours."

Kyra didn't have a chance to talk to Jake the rest of the day, and he'd be spending his evening with his daughter. Would Fiona admit to her father that she'd been the one who'd given her mom a heads-up about Kyra's lurid past? Kyra thought Fiona might welcome her relationship with her father to get him off her case while she stayed with him. She'd underestimated the girl.

Kyra finished her work at the station, conducted her group session at the office and headed home to change before visiting Quinn. He'd tried to protect her for so long, but a shifting world of quick internet searches, hacking and social media had made that impossible—even for him.

She put on a pair of jeans, a T-shirt and sneakers. On her way out the door, she grabbed a hoodie. When she reached Quinn's house in Venice, the sun had already dipped halfway into the ocean and a damp marine layer had started seeping into the canals, the moist droplets it brought clinging to her eyelashes and the loose strands of her hair.

She possessed a key, but she knocked on Quinn's door out of courtesy. As it got harder and harder for him to move around, she hated calling him to the front door. "It's me, Quinn."

"C'mon in."

She used her key and poked her head inside the house. "Smells good. I didn't bring a thing with me. I was in a rush."

"I already told you—" he waved a spoon in the air

from the kitchen "—Rose provided everything the other day. She even dropped off homemade bread."

"Rose is working hard to impress you, Quinn. I hope you invited her to share the stew with you when she brought it over."

"Of course, I did. What do you take me for? You're getting the leftovers, but if Rose's trying to replace Charlotte, it's just not gonna happen." He dropped the spoon and held his arms wide. "Now, get over here."

She let her bag slip to the floor and practically skipped across the living room to the kitchen. Wrapping her arms around Quinn's waist, she rested her head against his shoulder, and he stroked her hair as he used to do when she was a kid running away from her latest disaster of a foster home.

After the support and acceptance of her colleagues at the station and the warm emails from her clients, she hadn't realized how much she needed this comfort from Quinn. He was the only one who could truly understand.

More than ten years of a carefully crafted identity shattered by a blog post.

Quinn wasn't as sturdy as he used to be, though, and he'd staggered back a bit under the enthusiasm of her greeting. She pulled away from him and kissed his weathered cheek. "Thanks for getting it."

"I know the revelations didn't hurt you professionally, Mimi—may have even helped—but I don't like it." He turned away from her and grabbed two bowls.

"I know you don't, Quinn." She patted his back. "But even if The Player is still alive and paying attention to all this, he has no reason to come for me. He got away with murder, several murders. He's not going to risk anything now."

"You'd better believe if he's alive, he's paying attention." He picked up the spoon from the sink and shook it under her nose, sending droplets of gravy flying onto his white cabinets. "Are you kidding? He's probably following these copycats with breathless excitement."

She hated it when Quinn talked about The Player as if he were a part of their lives. He was imprisoned or dead. He meant nothing to her today.

"Be careful with that thing." Reaching around Quinn, she picked up a dish sponge from the sink and ran it under the faucet. Then she dabbed at the spots on his cabinets. "The Player might be salivating over all the death in his name, but he has nothing to do with me."

"I know. Don't pay any attention to the old man rambling in the corner about his one failure." Quinn took two steps around her with the bowls in his hands and set them down next to the stove, where a pot simmered and emitted mouthwatering aromas from its bubbling depths.

"Let me fill those. Take the bread and have a seat." She took the ladle from his hand and dipped it into the stew. When she'd filled the bowls, she brought them to the table, where they joined slices of crusty bread. "It almost feels like fall around here."

Holding up a can of beer, Quinn said, "I don't have any wine for you."

"That's okay. You'd think I'd be dying for a few drinks after getting outed by Sean Hughes, but everything went surprisingly well." She spread butter on a piece of warm bread, and it soaked in immediately.

"If it hadn't gone well for you at the station, they would've had me to answer to—Castillo knows that."

"Captain Castillo?" She bit into the bread.

Quinn reddened to the roots of his silver hair and shoved a spoonful of stew into his mouth.

Kyra brushed the crumbs from her fingers onto the bread plate. "Has Castillo known my identity all this time?"

Quinn swallowed and patted his lips with a napkin, covering the lower half of his face. "He's the only one. I didn't tell him. He just…knew."

"Makes sense." She shrugged. "He was around then. He worked on the case, didn't he?"

"He did."

"Is that why…?" She stirred the chunky contents of her bowl. "Never mind. There was one roadblock to my happiness today."

"Not Jake, he already knew. Why would he be upset?"

"His ex-wife."

Quinn clutched the handle of his spoon with a curled fist. "What did she have to say about it, and how'd she find out? She doesn't even live here, does she?"

"She lives up north, Monterey."

Quinn's spoon clinked against the bowl as he dropped it. "It was his daughter, huh?"

"I'm pretty sure she told her mother all about the woman her dad is dating." Kyra twisted her lips and took a sip of water.

"Don't worry about it." Quinn reached over and patted her hand. "As a therapist, you know it's not unusual for kids to sabotage their parents' dating lives. You never had to resort to that because Charlotte and I presented a united front at all times—even if we weren't all that united behind the scenes, sometimes, but as you never lived with us, you never saw any of that."

"It doesn't surprise me, but the ex took it to heart and called Jake to read him the riot act about me." She left off the part where Tess had referred to her as a *killer*. Quinn didn't need to hear that.

"You and Jake can cool it while his daughter's here. You were going to do that anyway, right? Then the ex will come around, and the daughter will come around, and the two of you can get married and start a family of your own."

Kyra choked on the bread in her mouth and had to wash it down with water. "Is that what you have planned for me?"

Quinn's faded blue eyes softened. "Why not? I like Jake. I trust Jake. He can take care of you when I'm gone."

That was the second time Quinn had mentioned Jake taking care of her.

She sealed her lips. Quinn wouldn't want to be reminded that she took care of him a lot more than he took care of her these days. "You're not going anywhere, and I can take care of myself. Isn't that why you taught me to use a gun?"

"Don't get your hackles up. I know you can handle yourself, but there's nothing wrong with having someone on your side while you do it. Charlotte and I took care of each other—until the end."

"I know you did." She sniffed and scooped up another spoonful of stew to blame it on the steam rising from the bowl. She and Quinn hadn't gotten so sentimental since Charlotte's passing a few years back.

"How'd that blogger get your story? Aren't the Department of Children and Family Services records confidential anymore?" Quinn ripped apart a piece of bread as if it were Sean Hughes's body.

"You know they are. It's different today, Quinn. People get access to records in all kinds of ways—some of them illegal."

He waved the bread at her and the crumbs showered the tablecloth. "Even I know about that *LA Confidential* blog. He's anti law enforcement."

"I wouldn't say that." She shoved the remaining contents of her bowl around, delaying dropping the next shoe for Quinn. "He's interested in crime. He's interested in law enforcement. He calls out injustices."

"There's no injustice in an officer like Jansen working undercover. He was with a hard-core biker gang who could've killed him."

"To give Sean credit, he didn't reveal Jansen's identity until his assignment ended."

"Don't like it."

"Then you're really not going to like this. The LAPD has decided to use Sean's blog as a channel of communication between Jake and Copycat Three."

Quinn snorted beer out of his nose and made a grab for his napkin. "Is that what they're calling him?"

"It's going to make him angry."

"Must've been your idea."

"It was."

He dragged the napkin across his nose and dropped it in his lap. "I can understand why you'd want to use the blog, but it doesn't sit right with me. Still, I'm glad Jake has a vehicle to reach out to the killer. Copycat Three has an ego, and it'll trip him up."

"The response will needle him, for sure." She placed her bowl on top of her bread plate. "Thank Rose for me. I'll clean up, and then if you don't mind, I'll keep you company for a while. I'm in no hurry to get home."

He cocked an eyebrow at her. "Will I be seeing more of you with Jake's daughter in town?"

"Can't I just like your company?"

"I know you do, Mimi." He pushed back from the table with some difficulty, but she refrained from helping him. There was only so much assistance a man like Quinn would take. "I'll rinse and you can put the dishes in the dishwasher."

"That's a deal."

When she finished washing up the cookware, she joined Quinn in the living room where an old Hitchcock film played on the TV. She curled up in the corner of the sofa and dragged out her laptop.

Jake had texted her a couple of times during the evening and assured her he'd made some progress with his ex-wife. She just hoped he wasn't pushing things with Fiona.

She accessed *LA Confidential* and read more comments on Sean's blog about her history. He was already teasing the story for tomorrow, and despite her excitement about it a little knot had formed in her gut.

It was one thing to hunt a nameless, faceless, anonymous killer and quite another to have contact with that killer. It made the search for him that much more…personal.

She blew out a breath and took a sip of hot tea. Jake could take care of himself a lot better than she could take care of herself. If she thought Quinn's worries about her were absurd, Jake would laugh off her concerns about him.

She glanced at Quinn over the top of her laptop, and then brought up Websleuths. "Quinn, have you ever heard of these true crime message boards where people discuss missing persons and murders?"

"I've heard about them." He paused the movie. "One of them played a role in the investigation of the Golden State Killer, although more in the way of speculation than hard evidence. I suppose they're all chattering about these copycat killings."

"I suppose so. I've glanced through a few of them, and people really do want to help. It's not just ghoulish rubbernecking."

Jake had shared a lot about the case with Quinn, but he hadn't told him about the link between copycats one and two and the Websleuths site. She'd honor that—especially because she had her own interest in the site now.

Holding her breath, she clicked on her personal messages on the website. Toby Dog had responded to her, and she read his message with a hand clenched against her belly. Weird, but not serial killer recruitment level weird.

He and his special friends liked to take the action from the message boards to *real life*, as he called it. They traveled to the crime sites, they did investigative work like measuring distances and time, visited the locations where the victims were last seen.

The administrators of the website prohibited that kind of activity, and if they found out a member was conducting his or her own investigation, they'd ban that member from the website.

She had no desire to play supersleuth, but Toby Dog, which she'd figured out was the name of Sherlock Holmes's dog, piqued her curiosity about whether or not members were engaged in this activity on the copycat killer message board. What could they find out that the police couldn't?

As she clicked in the field to respond, her phone rang. She caught her breath as she saw Sean's name pop up on the display. She hoped he wasn't having a change of heart.

As she answered, she pushed the laptop from her

legs and stood up. "Hope you haven't changed your mind."

Quinn looked up from his movie, and she waved him off as she sauntered out to his front porch.

Sean's heavy breathing made him sound like a creeper or as if he'd just finished running a 5k. "I haven't changed my mind, but I need to talk to you about something—in person."

"Are you all right? You sound…out of breath."

"I am a little, but I'm okay. Can you meet me?"

"Now?" With her belly full of stew and sourdough bread, she didn't feel like hopping on the freeway to meet with a blogger about last-minute changes.

He answered in clipped tones. "Yes, now."

"Do you want me to bring Jake?"

"Just you. It's important, Kyra."

Her hands suddenly turned clammy. "Is—is this about the blog tomorrow or the blog today?"

"Both. It has to be just you. I need to meet you now, or I'm not going to be able to post the blog tomorrow."

She glanced through the window at Quinn enthralled by Grace Kelly. He'd always told her that her mother had gotten it all wrong. Instead of naming her Marilyn after Marilyn Monroe, she should've named her Grace. Marilyn or Grace, he wouldn't want her running off to meet Sean Hughes in the middle of the night.

"Kyra?"

"I—I'm still here. Where are you? At your home?" She had no idea where Sean lived, but anyone calling

LA home could live a good forty-five minutes away from every other place in LA.

"I'm not at my house, but I live in Echo Park and I can meet you at the park by the lake there."

"Why there? Can't we meet at a bar or coffee-house?"

"No!" Sean took a few steadying breaths. "We can't be seen together. This is important, Kyra. Do you want that blog to run tomorrow?"

"It has to."

"Then I'll see you when you get here. There are still people walking on the path around the lake. I'll be waiting in my black BMW in the parking lot near the little boat dock for those swan pedal boats. You know the area?"

"I know it." She checked the time on her phone. "I'm in Venice. If there's no traffic, I'll be there in about thirty minutes. This better be good."

Sean hung up without responding, and Kyra slipped inside Quinn's house.

He looked up. "Everything okay?"

"Everything's fine, but I have a work thing and I need to get going."

Quinn studied her for a few seconds, and she marched past him to grab her hoodie. She brushed a kiss against his cheek. "I'll see you next time."

Grabbing her hand, he said, "Be careful."

"I always am." She moved her hand over the gun pouch on the side of her purse.

As she drove north to Echo Park, she periodically glanced at her phone to make sure Sean hadn't texted her to call off the meeting or decide he could tell her everything over the phone. A few times, she'd reached for her cell to call Jake, but she didn't want to intrude on his father-daughter time or worry him about his response getting posted tomorrow.

Had Sean discovered something about his anonymous source that he wanted to reveal to her? That would be the best scenario. She'd convinced herself that Sean's source was her nemesis, Laprey, the person who'd been toying with her ever since the copycat killings began with Jordy Lee Cannon.

Laprey was more than a prankster, if he were responsible for the homeless woman's death. He could've even been culpable in her foster brother's overdose. That would leave two bodies at his door.

The drive took her closer to forty minutes than thirty, and by the time she swung into the parking lot near the boat dock only two cars remained—Sean's and a white truck—both looked empty.

She parked next to Sean's car and strapped her purse across her chest as she exited her vehicle. Lights along the edge of the lot saved it from complete darkness, and the moon lit up the swan boats bumping and swaying on the water.

"Sean?" She circled his car and stopped next to the driver's side. The dome light glowed inside, and she noticed that Sean had left the door ajar. A file folder had spilled its contents onto the floor of the car.

Kyra licked her dry lips and called Sean on her cell phone. As his phone rang, a buzzing noise emanated from his car. She peeked into the window and saw a light from beneath the driver's seat. Sean had left his phone in the car.

Swallowing, Kyra stepped back from the car and called out. "Sean?"

Had he decided to take a stroll while waiting for her? Why leave his phone behind and his car door open?

Kyra eyed the truck on the other side of the small parking lot, and unzipped her gun pouch as she crept toward it. Unlike Sean, the truck's owner had locked things up. Instinct or curiosity made her snap a picture of the truck's license plate with her phone.

Claiming a spot in the middle of the parking lot, she turned in a circle. The road wound away from the parking lot on one side, and the lake beckoned on the other. Maybe he had gone to check out the boats.

She glanced over her shoulder and made her way to the boat dock where the pedal boats floated in a corral. As they bumped together, the soft clicking noise sounded like chatter.

Her sneakers whispered against the dirt and gravel that bordered the man-made lake. She tripped to a stop as she noticed a huddled form at the edge of the water.

"Sean? Is that you?" She flicked on her phone's flashlight and rested her hand against her weapon, still zipped in her purse.

She drew closer to the man and a strangled scream clawed its way up her throat.

Sean Hughes lay curled on his side with a bullet hole in his head.

Chapter Eight

Jake's unmarked sedan squealed to a stop in the parking lot of Echo Park Lake. *She's okay. She's okay.* He repeated the mantra in his head as he threw his vehicle into Park and scrambled from the car.

His gaze darted around the scene, flooded with lights from the emergency vehicles, and landed on Kyra sitting in the back of an ambulance, her legs hanging over the end. The blood pounded against his temples as he strode toward her.

"Are you all right? Why are you in the ambulance?" He rushed to her side and put his hand against her cheek, as if that could verify her condition.

Her wide eyes sought his face. "He's dead. Sean Hughes is dead."

Jake dropped to his knees in front of her and clasped both of her hands in his. "I know that, but what are you doing here?"

"I warned him." Kyra's head twisted to the side where Sean's body lay crumpled beside the edge of the lake. "I warned him about his anonymous source."

The EMT standing next to them cleared his throat.

"You're okay, Kyra, but you might want to keep warm. You're still shivering from the shock."

"Do you want to sit in my car?" Jake squeezed her hands as another tremble rolled through her body.

"Do you have to look at the body?"

"Another detective is checking it out now. I'll have a look before the coroner gets here." He leaned forward and whispered, "First, I want to know what you were doing here."

She blinked. "Do you…do you think I had something to do with Sean's death? Is that what they think? Revenge for the blog?"

"That's just dumb. Do you really believe I'd think that?" He cinched her wrists and tugged her from the back of the ambulance. "I want to hear from you what happened."

Under his guidance, she hopped to the ground. "I already told the patrol officer. I haven't spoken to Detective Villareal, yet."

"You can give a statement to me, and I'll give it to Manny Villareal." Still holding her hand, he led her to his car. When he got into the driver's seat, he buzzed down the window in case someone wanted him…or Kyra. He turned to her. "Why the hell were you with Sean Hughes in a deserted park in the middle of the night?"

"He called me." She dug into her purse and withdrew her cell phone. She tapped her display and held it out to him to prove her statement. "There's the call at 8:52."

"I believe you, Kyra." He pushed the phone back in her direction. "What did he want?"

"This." She flung her arm out to the side and hit the window with the ring she wore on her right hand. "He asked me to meet him here to discuss the blog. He basically told me if I didn't come, he couldn't guarantee your response to Copycat Three would be posted tomorrow."

"He wouldn't tell you anything else?"

"No, and I asked. He insisted that we talk in person. I even asked why we couldn't meet in a coffee-house or bar, but he didn't want to be seen in public with me." She lifted her shoulders to her ears and held them there stiffly. "I don't know why, but I wasn't going to take a chance that he wouldn't post your response."

Jake reached over and massaged the back of her neck until she dropped her shoulders. "Did he sound…different?"

"I don't know him that well. I've spoken to him only a few times on the phone before this, but yeah, he sounded a little different."

Jake tensed. "How?"

"You heard him on speakerphone the other day. He's…he was a confident, smooth guy." She twisted her fingers in her lap. "This time…not so much. He sounded worried. His voice had an urgency. It lit a fire under me, anyway."

"Why?" Jake smacked the heel of his hand against his forehead. "Why would you agree to meet him here, of all places, in the dead of night?"

"You keep saying that—dead of night, middle of the night. It was nine o'clock. Even he told me there were people still walking around the lake." She grabbed his arm. "Did the police check out that white truck? That was the only other car in the lot besides Sean's car. I even took a picture of it, just in case."

"I'm sure they ran the plate. If it's anything or anyone connected, we'll hear about it, but I doubt a killer's going to leave his vehicle at the scene of the crime."

"Cameras?"

"They're here, and we'll find out soon enough."

"Even if the cameras don't catch the killer, the footage should at least rule me out."

He tucked an errant strand of hair behind her ear. "Nobody's ruling you in, but why did you take a picture of the truck's license plate? Did you suspect something was off? Take it from the top. You got the call. I'll bet you didn't tell Quinn where you were going and what you were doing."

"Of course not." She took a deep, steadying breath. "After Sean's call, I told Quinn I had something to do for work—which is true. It took me about forty minutes to get here—traffic on the 110 as I went through downtown. By the time I arrived, there were no more walkers or joggers in the park. I saw Sean's car and the truck. What gave me pause was that Sean's car door was ajar and his phone was on the floor under the driver's seat. That's why I approached the truck with caution. Then I walked toward the swan boats, and I saw Sean's body. That's it. I called 911."

"Why didn't you call me?"

"You heard the EMT. I was in shock. After I found Sean, I ran back to my car and sat there with the doors locked and my gun in my hand, in case the killer came back for me."

"I didn't mean after you found the body. I meant after you got the call from Sean."

"I didn't want to interrupt you, especially after what your ex said about me today."

Jake massaged his temples. "Did you tell the police about your gun?"

"No."

"You need to do that. They're going to want to know you had a weapon." Kyra's knees started bouncing, and he put a hand on one and squeezed. "They can rule out your gun as the murder weapon. Did they check your hands for gunshot residue, yet?"

"No."

"I'm going to suggest they do that, too."

"So, you *do* think they suspect me."

"They would be bad detectives if they didn't. You found the body, you had a motive, and they're going to discover that you had the means."

"And I called 911."

"You should know by now it's not unusual for the perpetrator to call in the crime." He stroked her hair. "I'm not trying to scare you. All of those things will rule you out."

"He killed him, Jake."

He chose his words carefully. "You think Laprey is his source, and Laprey killed him?"

"Yes." She pursed her lips and her jaw formed a firm line.

"Why would he do that? Why give Sean the story, and then get rid of him?"

"Maybe he thought Sean was going to reveal his source to me and I'd finally learn Laprey's identity."

"If Sean were going to do that, why not just tell you over the phone? How would Laprey know Sean hadn't already told you?"

"I'm not sure about all that, but who else would want to kill Sean? Kill him right before he talked to me?"

"Kill him when he knew you'd find the body."

Kyra had been a bundle of action ever since dropping into the passenger seat. Now all motion ceased. Her next words came out through gritted teeth. "What do you mean?"

"Maybe this was some kind of setup for you. Lure you out here to find Sean's dead body, maybe even an attempt to implicate you in Sean's death."

"But Sean called me out here."

"Did he?"

"Of course, he did. I haven't spoken to Sean much, but I did recognize his voice, and he called me from the number I have identified as his." She dragged a hand through her hair. "What are you suggesting, Detective?"

Jake drummed his fingers against the dashboard. "You said Sean sounded nervous on the phone, agitated. Maybe someone was forcing him to call you."

Kyra sucked in a quick breath. "You mean Sean's

life was already in danger when he called me? Someone was holding a gun to his head—literally or figuratively—to get him to call me and get me out here?"

"Then he killed Sean, and left the body here for you to find."

"Why wouldn't he stick around to kill me, too? He had the perfect opportunity."

"Think about it, Kyra." He waved a hand out the open window at Manny. "When has Laprey ever wanted to harm you? Tease you? Taunt you? Terrify you? Oh, yeah. All that. But he's never once threatened you with physical danger."

"What *does* he want?"

"Better question is who is he?" He opened his door. "I'm going to talk to Manny. I suggest you come with me if you feel up to it."

"I'm fine."

He waited for her, and they walked up to Manny together. "I took her statement, Manny. I'll write it up for you and email it, but Kyra has something she wants to tell you."

Detective Villareal, who'd just made detective last month, raised his eyebrows. "What is it, Ms. Chase?"

"You can call me Kyra." She unzipped the gun pouch on her purse and pulled out her weapon. "I did want to let you know that I have a gun. You're welcome to take it."

Manny assessed the gun with an expert eye and sniffed the barrel. "No need. We're looking for a .45, not a .22, and your gun hasn't been fired recently. Go see the guy in the blue shirt over by the crime scene tape. We have a portable sensor for gunshot residue and he can swab your hands now. Is that okay?"

"That's fine. If after reading Jake's... Detective McAllister's report, you have any questions for me, I'd be happy to talk with you. Unfortunately, I didn't see anything except the white truck."

"We know that belongs to someone who came here earlier, met his girlfriend, and the two of them took off in her car."

Jake nudged Kyra's back. "Go see Thomas to get your hands swabbed."

She nodded, correctly sensing he wanted to talk to Manny by himself.

When she'd created enough space between them, Jake turned to Manny. "Any witnesses? Anyone see Hughes here earlier?"

"We'll put out a call to the public, also ask if any-one has video or pictures on their phone from earlier this evening." Manny adjusted his tie and straight-ened his jacket. "The cameras are a no-go."

"They don't work?" Jake glanced up at the camera affixed to a lamppost.

Manny pointed skyward. "This one doesn't work, and the other one is at an angle that's not going to catch the action over here. Do you think the killer knew that?"

"Possibly, unless he's the one who broke the cam-era. Is it physically disabled?"

"No. Hasn't been working for a while. What's the point of having cameras if you don't verify they're working?"

Jake clapped Manny on the back. "Welcome to my world. And if the jacket and tie get to be too much, especially at a night scene like this, you can chuck 'em in the car."

"Good to know." Manny loosened his tie. "This is the guy who's posting your reply to the copycat killer, isn't he?"

"Interesting, huh?"

"Do you think the killer found out somehow and killed him before he could post it?"

"Good thought, but I think the killer is hoping I'll reply."

Manny's gaze shifted to Kyra, holding her hands out for Thomas as he passed the electrode over her skin. "He's also the blogger who released that stuff about Kyra's background."

"One and the same, but Kyra was cool with it. She's the one who contacted Hughes about posting my reply to the killer. He called her out here for a meeting, not the other way around. I saw a record of the phone call on her cell. Do you want her to turn it over to you?"

"She's not a suspect, but it would be too coincidental to believe Hughes's death isn't somehow related to his connection to the copycat killings."

"You'll make a good detective, Manny. Now it's up to you to figure out how it's related."

"I'm assuming the task force is going to follow my investigation closely."

"We'll be right beside you, brother."

Kyra waved and Thomas flashed them a thumbs-up.

Jake released a pent-up breath slowly through parted lips. "I guess that's it, then. Was Hughes shot point-blank or from a distance?"

"Point-blank. The killer may have forced Hughes from his car at gunpoint, led him to the water and shot him. Nobody around. Nobody heard a sound. We're hoping to round up some witnesses to find out if anyone saw Hughes here earlier. I understand when he called Kyra, he said there were people here."

"Could be. Could've been a lie to get her out here, make her feel safe."

They stopped talking as Kyra joined them. "No residue. Thomas will have it in a report."

As the coroner's van pulled into the parking lot, Jake said, "Wait for me in my car, unless Manny has any more questions for you. I'm going to take a quick look at the crime scene."

Jake strode toward the yellow tape and flashed his badge before ducking under it. One bullet to the back of the head. Maybe Hughes didn't know it was coming. Did someone force him out here? Force him to call Kyra? Did Hughes think he was setting up Kyra for her own death and not his?

Poor bastard. These laymen and amateur sleuths thought it was all fun and games—until a killer got you on his radar.

He finished examining the scene and returned to his car to find Kyra propped up against the hood. "Detective Villareal asked me a few more questions, but I don't think I'm on his short list."

"He doesn't have a list, but you wouldn't be on it,

anyway." He jerked his thumb over his shoulder at Sean's body. "I'm sorry you had to see that."

"It's not my first rodeo. I've seen dead bodies before, but I'm not gonna lie. This was a shock." She crossed her arms and dug her fingers into her biceps. "Are the cameras going to help?"

"The one in position doesn't work."

Her jaw dropped. "You're kidding me? What are the odds?"

"The odds that it's a coincidence? Not good." He brushed her arm with his knuckles. "Do you want to get in the car with me and talk some more, or are you ready to call it a night?"

"I'm more than ready to call it a night. I suppose I'm going to have to tell Quinn about this and suffer his wrath." She hitched her purse onto her shoulder and pushed off the car.

Clasping his hand on the back of his neck, Jake said, "I'm worried this is Laprey continuing his escalation. If he killed that homeless woman last month and now this, we know what he's capable of."

"We just don't know why he's targeting me. I'm assuming he found out about my past from Matt, my foster brother. Maybe he's just someone Matt knew and picked up on my story to blackmail me."

Jake said, "But he's never threatened to blackmail you."

"I don't know. Maybe it's someone who gets his kicks torturing and controlling women. Matt was in prison and hung out with some bad characters. It could be someone he met there."

"I'm going to start looking into that." He grabbed the car door and yanked it open. "I'd give you a big, long kiss right here and now if we didn't have an audience."

"An audience of your co-workers." She blew him a kiss from her fingertips. "Will that suffice?"

"It'll tide me over until I get you in my arms again. You don't know how scared I was when I got the call that you were in Echo Park with a dead Sean Hughes." He squeezed his eyes closed for a second, opening them when he felt Kyra's touch on his shoulder.

"Knowing they called you and you were on your way was the only thing that kept me together." She turned to go and stopped. Without looking around, she said, "We have to find another way to get out your response to Copycat Three."

"We'll figure out something." Jake slid behind the wheel and left his door open as he watched Kyra walk to her car, her head bent over her phone.

His heart jumped when Kyra stopped suddenly and spun around, her face a white oval in the darkness. Without even thinking, he jumped from the car and made a beeline to Kyra, still frozen, her feet rooted to the asphalt.

Lunging toward her, he asked, "What's wrong?"

"I—I got a message from Sean's phone I didn't see before."

"What did he say? Is it a clue about his killer?"

"I don't think Sean sent this message." She turned the phone toward him and it said, "I did it for you."

YOU pick your books –
WE pay for everything.

You get up to FOUR New Books and
TWO Mystery Gifts...absolutely FREE

Dear Reader,

I am writing to announce the launch of a huge **FREE BOOKS GIVEAWAY**... and to let you know that YOU are entitled to choose up to FOUR fantastic books that WE pay for.

Try **Harlequin® Romantic Suspense** books featuring heart-racing page-turners with unexpected plot twists and irresistible chemistry that will keep you guessing to the very end.

Try **Harlequin Intrigue® Larger-Print** books featuring action-packed stories that will keep you on the edge of your seat. Solve the crime and deliver justice at all costs. family and community unite.

Or **TRY BOTH!**

In return, we ask just one favor: Would you please participate in our brief Reader Survey? We'd love to hear from you.

This FREE BOOKS GIVEAWAY means that we pay for everything! We'll even cover the shipping, and no purchase is necessary, now or later. So please return your survey today.

You'll get **Two Free Books** and **Two Mystery Gifts** from each series to try, altogether worth over **$20!**

Sincerely

Pam Powers

Pam Powers
For Harlequin Reader Service

Complete the survey below and return it today to receive up to 4 FREE BOOKS and FREE GIFTS guaranteed!

FREE BOOKS GIVEAWAY
Reader Survey

1

Do you prefer stories with suspenseful storylines?

○ YES ○ NO

2

Do you share your favorite books with friends?

○ YES ○ NO

3

Do you often choose to read instead of watching TV?

○ YES ○ NO

YES! Please send me my Free Rewards, consisting of **2 Free Books from each series I select** and Free Mystery Gifts. I understand that I am under no obligation to buy anything, as explained on the back of this card.

❑ **Harlequin® Romantic Suspense** (240/340 HDL GQ56)
❑ **Harlequin Intrigue® Larger-Print** (199/399 HDL GQ56)
❑ **Try Both** (240/340 & 199/399 HDL GQ6J)

FIRST NAME

LAST NAME

ADDRESS

APT.#

CITY

STATE/PROV.

ZIP/POSTAL CODE

EMAIL ❑ Please check this box if you would like to receive newsletters and promotional emails from Harlequin Enterprises ULC and its affiliates. You can unsubscribe anytime.

HI/HRS-520-FBG/THF21

HARLEQUIN Reader Service — **Here's how it works:**

▲ If offer card is missing write to: Harlequin Reader Service, P.O. Box 1341, Buffalo, NY 14240-8531 or visit www.ReaderService.com ▲

BUSINESS REPLY MAIL
FIRST-CLASS MAIL   PERMIT NO. 717   BUFFALO, NY

POSTAGE WILL BE PAID BY ADDRESSEE

HARLEQUIN READER SERVICE
PO BOX 1341
BUFFALO NY 14240-8571

NO POSTAGE
NECESSARY
IF MAILED
IN THE
UNITED STATES

Chapter Nine

Confusion crisscrossed Jake's face, but Kyra knew exactly what the message meant and who had sent it. She swallowed the lump in her throat. "It's him, Jake. It's Laprey. He sent this message from Sean's phone before…or after he killed him."

"The timing of it is going to be important to the investigation. Is he trying to pretend he killed Sean Hughes to avenge you when, in all probability, he's the one who leaked your story to Sean?"

She clasped the phone to her thundering heart. "It's just another way to manipulate me. What does he want? Who *is* he?"

"Let's take your phone to Manny. They're gonna see that text to you once they get into Sean's phone, anyway." Jake curled an arm around her waist and led her back to the crime scene when she'd just wanted to escape it all.

Thirty minutes later, Jake walked her back to her car. "Are you sure you're going to be okay tonight? You can stay with me and to hell with Tess."

She put her hands on his strong shoulders. "It's not

just Tess. It's Fiona, too. I'll be fine. Like you pointed out earlier, he's never tried to physically harm me. In his mind he just killed for me."

"He's obsessed with you. We both know how quickly obsession can turn to violence."

She ground her back teeth to suppress the shiver creeping up her spine. "Maybe, but not tonight. I'll call you when I get to my apartment."

Jake finally let her go, worry creasing his handsome face. He followed her out of the parking lot, and his headlights stayed glued behind her until she reached her freeway where she peeled off from him.

Had Laprey been watching her in that parking lot? No, he wouldn't have stayed around for the police. Was Jake right? Had Sean's killer forced him to call her? Had he been listening to their conversation when Sean called her, to make sure Sean didn't give anything away?

This murder would make the news tomorrow, and the stories would drag her name through it all—even more reason for Tess to want to keep her far, far away from Fiona. Kyra didn't blame her.

She got home well past midnight and didn't even feel silly clutching her gun in her hand from the car to her apartment. If it got down to it, she knew she could protect herself as long as someone didn't surprise her. She had no intention of being taken by surprise.

Spot, the stray cat, didn't make an appearance to greet her, so she shut and secured her front door. Jake had mentioned cameras for her apartment, and now might be the time to act on that.

When she crawled into bed, she plugged her phone into the charger and cradled it in the palm of her hand. She studied the text message, from Sean's phone but not from Sean. Detective Villareal had discovered that the message must've been scheduled earlier and sent from a message app on the phone, as the delivery time was after the discovery of Sean's body. It had given her some comfort that she hadn't missed the message.

This was the first communication she'd had from Laprey since he sent her the email with the picture of her foster family, threatening to expose the fact that she'd stabbed her foster father to death after he'd been molesting the younger girls in the home and had attacked her for trying to protect one of the girls.

Jake had discovered the truth, anyway, and now the whole world knew about it, thanks to Sean Hughes… and his source. Laprey's harassment of her had begun during the reign of the first copycat killer, Jordy Cannon. It had continued and escalated during Cyrus Fisher's killing spree, and now had come to a head with this third killer.

Did Laprey know these killers? Was he working in coordination with them? Or had he been holding on to this information and decided to torment her with it when the killings started?

Her foster brother, Matt Dugan, had been involved with Laprey somehow. She and Jake had discovered Laprey's name among Matt's possessions when he died. In fact, several people involved with Laprey had wound up dead. Would she be next? Was that his endgame?

Sighing, she placed the phone on the nightstand and dragged her pillow beneath her head. Tomorrow, she and Jake needed to start working on another vehicle for his response to Copycat Three. She couldn't let her own problems derail her from her work with the task force, but once again she couldn't shake the feeling that the current killings involved her...and the man who had murdered her mother twenty years ago.

HER PHONE BUZZED, and Kyra opened one eye, sticky with sleep. She peered at the display before answering. "How did you manage to wake up so early after the night we had?"

Jake said, "It's not that early. I tried calling you before and got worried when you didn't answer."

Holding her phone away from her, she said, "Looks like I missed a few calls this morning. I hear background noise. Are you at the station already?"

"Yes, and I have big news for you."

She shot up, banging the back of her head against the headboard. "What is it?"

"Sean must've scheduled his blog to post today because it's out this morning, and you were right—it's creating a buzz."

"It must be creating an even bigger buzz with Sean's death." She threaded her fingers through her hair and rubbed her scalp. "Are news sources making the connection between the post and his murder last night?"

"Speculation is running rampant, and the blog is getting a lot of eyes. Copycat Three would have to be living in a cave to miss it."

"For all we know, he *might* be living in a cave. You don't have much on him." She switched Jake to speaker and hopped onto the internet, bringing up *LA Confidential.* "I'm looking at it now. I'm just sorry Sean's not around to enjoy the results."

"How are you feeling this morning?"

"Tired, but more energized now that I know all our work with Sean wasn't in vain and we don't have to start over. This is good. This is really good." She threw back the covers and planted her bare feet on the carpet. "How's everyone on the task force taking it?"

"It's like a roller coaster around here. People are shocked by Hughes's murder and excited by his blog."

"I suppose everyone knows Sean called me and that I found the body." Holding the phone in one hand, Kyra shuffled to her bathroom and frowned at the circles under her eyes.

"Everyone knows." Jake cleared his throat. "You don't have to come into the station today."

"Of course I do. What do you take me for?" She flicked back her hair and cranked on the shower. "I'm not responsible for Sean's death. Did Villareal release the text message I got?"

"Nope. That's something we're going to keep to ourselves. I'll let you go. It sounds like you're in a wind tunnel."

"That's the shower. I'll see you when I get in." She placed the phone on the vanity and pulled her nightgown over her head. "I suppose this latest news is going to give your ex-wife even more ammunition against me."

"Don't worry about Tess. I can make her see reason."

They ended the call and Kyra stepped beneath the warm spray of the shower. She didn't want to tell Jake, but it wasn't Tess that concerned her—it was his daughter.

Later that morning, Kyra tried to slip into the task force war room as unobtrusively at possible, but she didn't have to worry because Detective Villareal came in and swooped her up for more questioning as soon as she walked through the door.

She ran through the timeline with him again and showed him her phone. He confirmed the scheduling app the killer had used to send her the message from Sean's phone. He also told her there had been several calls between Sean's phone and a burner phone.

As they wrapped things up, she asked, "Did you find any witnesses who were there earlier and might have seen Sean and his killer?"

"We have a few people coming in later who were at the lake, but I think Sean was lying to you about people at the lake. It wasn't very crowded. We checked with the security company who monitors the footage from the cameras—when they're working—and the folks there told us traffic to the lake falls off this time of the year. The kids are back in school and the end of daylight saving time keeps people away. Sean…

or someone else was trying to give you a false sense of security."

"I'll ask my friend, Megan Wright, a reporter from KTOP, where Sean might've kept information about his sources. I suppose you confiscated his computer."

"We did." Villareal's dark eyes flashed. "It's a good thing Hughes scheduled that blog before he died. Now it's getting more attention than ever. Of course, he couldn't have known at the time his murder would make the hits to his blog go through the roof."

"I wonder if the killer knew the blog was going to post anyway?" Kyra drew circles on the desk with her fingertip. "When I talked to Sean, he indicated to me the blog might not get published unless I met him at the park."

"It could've been his way to convince you to come out."

"Or he was hiding it from his killer. Maybe the guy killed Sean to stop him from posting Jake's response."

"Why would he care about that? His interest and focus were on you, not the copycats."

Kyra folded her hands to stop her restless fingers. "Detective Villareal, I'm sure you read about my past yesterday. I'm connected to the copycat killers in more ways than one."

He dropped his gaze, a habit he'd have to break if he expected to be a successful homicide detective. Victims' families didn't want a detective who was going to shy away from their pain and horror. If the cops couldn't take the heat, how were the victims' loved ones supposed to survive?

"I read about it, and I'm sorry. I guess that's how you know Quinn." He met her eyes again and curiosity had replaced uneasiness.

Better. "You know about Roger Quinn?"

"He's a legend. Who doesn't know about Quinn at the LAPD?"

"I'm sure he'll be thrilled to hear it." She didn't plan on discussing her and Quinn's relationship with Villareal. Scooting her chair back from the table, she said, "If that's all…"

"That's all for now, Kyra, and you can call me Manny."

"Thanks, Manny. Let me know if you need anything else from me."

On her way back to the task force room, Captain Castillo called out to her as she passed his office. She stuck her head into the room. "Captain?"

"Have a seat for a minute." He tapped a few keys on his laptop and then pushed it to the side. "Good work on that reply to Copycat Three. It hits all the right notes."

She sank into one of the comfy leather chairs on the other side of his desk and immediately felt like taking a nap. "I'm just glad it posted."

"I'm sorry about last night. That must've been… frightening, especially after the day you had yesterday."

"Yeah, it's been a whirlwind of emotions." She crossed one leg over the other and clasped her hands around one knee. Amid all the turmoil, she hadn't forgotten Quinn telling her last night that Castillo had known her identity all this time. "Captain Castillo, Quinn mentioned last night that you've always known about my past—that my mother, Jennifer Lake, was one of The Player's victims."

Castillo's eyes widened for a split second and Kyra read fear in their depths. Then his chin bobbed to his chest. "Guilty."

She raised her eyebrows. Was he apologizing to her? "Nothing to confess to. I guess I should've realized it, as you worked on the case and you knew Quinn. You would've known the saga of the poor little girl left an orphan after her mother's murder."

He bowed his head again, his gaze shifting away from hers. "What else did Quinn tell you?"

"Not much. He just sort of mentioned in passing that Sean Hughes's scoop wouldn't be news to you. I guess it didn't occur to me that even someone working on the case would've known about my name change."

"My wife and Charlotte Quinn were also friends."

"I suppose that makes sense. Is that why you threw work my way and made a place for me on the copycat task force?"

Castillo jerked, and his hands fluttered like an errant bird over the various items on his desk. "You think I hired you to appease Quinn? Absolutely not."

She tilted her head, and her ponytail slid over one shoulder. "That's not what I meant, although that could be a reason. You must've thought my unenviable position as the daughter of a murder victim would give me a unique perspective, especially on these cases that mimic The Player."

"Yes, that's it." He shook a finger at her, but his playful smile didn't reach his eyes. "I don't play favorites around here, Kyra. You're an asset to the team. Everyone thinks so, even the chief."

"Good to hear it."

"Now, if you'll excuse me. I have some phone calls to make. I just wanted to offer my condolences for your shock last night and my kudos for a job well done on that response for J-Mac."

"Thank you on both counts...and thanks for keeping my secret all these years." She rose from the chair and slipped out the door, shutting it behind her.

Holding her breath and tensing her muscles, she stood at the door and pressed her ear against the wood for several seconds. All remained quiet from inside Castillo's office. He hadn't picked up the phone. He was probably too busy collecting himself.

That was the oddest conversation she'd had since... well, since the conversation she'd had with Sean last night. What had Captain Castillo been so afraid of? Had he made some deal with Quinn to watch over her here at the station? Why would he worry if she discovered that? Quinn was the one who'd have to pay the price for that one.

She'd bring it up with Jake. The thought plastered a smile on her face. When she'd first met Jake, she'd kept him in the dark about everything, just like she'd always kept everyone at arm's length. Now she shared everything with him…almost everything. She hadn't told him yet about her foray onto Websleuths.

She flipped her ponytail over her shoulder. A girl had to keep some secrets.

When she finally collapsed at her desk in front of her laptop, the sounds of lunchtime stirred around her. A quick glance at Jake's desk assured her he had delved into something engrossing and wouldn't be coming up for air for a while. He hadn't even looked up when she entered the room. Plenty of other people had, though, and she'd become an even bigger object of curiosity than she'd been before.

She'd barely gotten through an email to the mother of Copycat Three's first victim, Juliana French, when her phone buzzed. She read the display and blew out a breath. She'd wondered how long it was going to take for Megan to call her.

Megan didn't even let her finish saying hello before she launched into an avalanche of words. "Oh my God. You were on my you-know-what list yesterday when I realized you had this bombshell story you never told me about, and then I found out you were going to use *LA Confidential* for Jake's reply to the killer instead of me, but now I'm so glad you did. Do you think Sean got killed because he revealed your true identity or because he was the go-between for J-Mac and the killer? Do the cops think Copycat Three offed Sean, or was it the source of your story or some other random person who had it in for him? And are you okay? My God, to stumble on a gruesome murder scene like that. I'm here if you need a margarita or seven."

"Take a breath." Kyra rolled her eyes. "First of all, I hadn't planned to reveal my past to anyone—bombshell or not. Secondly, Jake wanted to use a digital medium for his response. Thirdly, I'm fine and I could use several margaritas at some point, and I'll let you know when."

Megan scooped in an audible breath over the phone and Kyra braced for another onslaught, but Megan lowered her voice. "Seriously, I am so sorry Sean dragged you into whatever that was last night."

"And you're sorry about Sean."

"Live by the sword, die by the sword. The guy was always playing with fire." She coughed. "I mean, of course I'm sorry for Sean. Do you have a bone you can throw a sistah? Any details you can share that the cops aren't revealing about Sean's murder?"

Megan could take off running with the information that Sean's killer had texted Kyra, claiming he'd killed Sean for her, but the task force was keeping that to themselves for now and she wouldn't be the one to compromise the investigation.

"I don't have anything I can give you about that, Megan, but when things settle down, I'd be happy to give you an exclusive interview if you want it."

"If I want it? Yes, yes and yes. Let me know, and let me know when you're ready for those margaritas. They are not contingent on the interview."

"I know that."

When Kyra ended the call, someone tapped her on

the shoulder, and she glanced up into Jake's face. No one else she'd rather see right now.

She asked, "Are we having lunch?"

"As it seems it's the only time I get to see you, except for murder scenes, I'm counting on it. It's a late one, so can we make it a long one, too? I'm bleary-eyed from staring at the computer and Billy's knocked off early to meet with his PI, Dina."

"You must've been reading my mind. I'm thinking Mi Casa, booth in the back, a few stolen kisses."

"You must've been reading *my* mind." He jerked his thumb over his shoulder. "Just need to touch base with a few people. Meet you by my car."

Kyra logged off her computer and stashed it in her bag. If they had a long lunch, it might just turn into a work lunch. She gathered the rest of her things and walked out of the building, her gaze flicking to Captain Castillo's closed door as she passed it.

She scrolled through text messages on her phone until Jake showed up and unlocked the car with his remote. She was already seated and struggling with the seat belt when he got behind the wheel.

Cranking her head around, she asked, "When do you think we're going to hear from Copycat Three?"

"I hate to say it, but I think he'll communicate with me in the same way he did before." He backed up and pulled out of the parking lot of the Northeast Division.

"You mean, over someone's dead body." She'd finally clicked the seat belt into place and held on to the strap across her body.

"I'm afraid so."

"And you don't think he's going to kill someone just for the opportunity to taunt you again?"

"We already went through that possibility, didn't we? He's not going to stop, regardless. He already has the urge, and he's going to keep satisfying it until we put an end to his craving. He gave us an opening by leaving that note for me. I'm not going to squander that chance." Jake cranked up the AC, even though the sun had yet to make an appearance through the overcast sky. "I thought you were on board with that."

"I am." She rubbed the goose bumps on her arms. "I just can't help thinking about some woman going about her life today for maybe the last time."

"I know. Have you talked to Quinn yet about what happened last night?"

"He sent me a text asking if I was okay. He knows I'll spill everything in my own way and time." Her gaze slid to Jake's profile, still set in work mode. "I'm going to tell him about the text Sean's killer sent to me. He may have some thoughts on that, and you know he won't tell anyone."

"If you weren't going to tell him about it, I was. The more the killings relate to you and your situation, the more I want Quinn's insight."

She licked her lips. "Because you think the two are connected by more than opportunity. You think Laprey, the person tormenting me, is somehow related to the killers."

"I think so, Kyra. Does he know who the copycats are?" He shrugged. "I don't know about that, but he's following their deeds closely. He may be on the Web-sleuths site, as well."

Kyra gulped down her guilt. She should tell Jake she was trolling Websleuths. She tapped the window. "Next turn if we're going to Mi Casa."

"I *wish* we were going to *mi casa*." He reached over and ran a finger down the side of her neck to her shoulder. "I miss you."

"How's Fiona holding up? Getting all her school-work done?" Someone had to bring them back to reality.

"She's doing fine. I'm not sure why she was so desperate to come down here. She knew I had to work and wouldn't get to spend much time with her, unlike when she visits for Christmas. I think…" He drummed his thumbs against the steering wheel.

"You think that's probably why she did hightail it out of Monterey for LA. She could escape her mother, and she knew you wouldn't be around much. Win, win for Fiona."

"Sounds like you know my daughter better than I do."

He parked the car, and they easily got their dark booth in the corner of the half-empty restaurant.

Once they'd ordered, had their basket of chips be-tween them, two types of salsa and a couple of iced teas, Kyra brought up the subject that had been on her mind all afternoon. "I had an interesting talk with Captain Castillo this afternoon."

"I have very few interesting conversations with Castillo, but I shouldn't complain. He's not someone to force his views on a case. He's letting me and Billy run this task force with zero interference."

"Do you know that he was aware of my identity all this time?"

Jake dropped a chip back into the basket. "What? You're kidding."

"Quinn let it slip the other night. It surprised me, but I don't know why it should. He was working The Player case twenty years ago. He must've known that Quinn was the one who found me hiding in the closet in my mother's bedroom the night she was murdered. He knew of Quinn and Charlotte's interest in me. Castillo told me today that his wife and Charlotte were close, so he would've known about the Quinns' desire to adopt me and how they kept a close eye on me all those years."

"Makes sense. There's a lot that makes sense now." He scooped up a mound of salsa.

She cocked one eyebrow at him. "You mean why Castillo always seemed like my champion?"

"Yeah. Not that he doesn't think you're good at what you do. He does. Castillo may be unassuming, but he's not stupid. Just not sure he would've gone out on a limb like he did for you on several occasions if he didn't owe it to Quinn."

"You think Quinn strong-armed him into accepting me?" She tapped her chin, indicating where Jake had a spot of salsa.

He swiped a napkin across his face. "Did I say *strong-arm*? Don't get it into your head that Castillo threw you any bones. He wouldn't do that if he didn't think you were qualified—not even for Quinn."

"Castillo said the same thing to me." She twirled her straw through her tea, causing the ice to clink against the glass.

"But?"

"I don't know. His demeanor was weird."

"In what way?"

"When I brought up the subject, he seemed almost afraid."

"That makes sense." Jake cut off his explanation as the waiter delivered their food.

Kyra toyed with her tostada until the waiter finished refilling their tea and backed off. "Why does Castillo's fear make sense?"

"He was probably worried about saying the wrong thing to you and having that get back to Quinn."

She snorted and stabbed at a piece of chicken. "Quinn's not some ogre guarding me."

"Really? 'Cause I felt like I had to accomplish a bunch of daring deeds to be worthy of you in Quinn's eyes."

"You must've passed muster because Quinn has our future all planned out."

"He does, huh? I'm glad he's on my side because I kind of have our future all planned out, too."

Her cheeks burned and it wasn't the salsa. "We have to get past the objections of your ex-wife and daughter before we can do much planning."

"Tess doesn't have the right to call any shots. I didn't say a word when she decided to move up north with Brock, and take Fiona with her. I figured Fiona would be better off with a mother and a father figure who wasn't getting called out to gruesome crime scenes in the middle of the night. Tess will see reason eventually...and so will Fiona." He dragged a fork through his rice. "Fiona was actually very interested in you after finding out about your past."

"Yeah, well, I'm not sure that interest is healthy." Fiona wasn't the only one with unhealthy interests. Kyra took a deep breath and said, "You were bleary-eyed looking through Websleuths. Did you find anything?"

"Nothing from looking at the posts, not even looking at Cannon's and Fisher's posts, which are still up. We asked the site to leave them. If there's any communication going on, it must be through the private chats, and Cannon and Fisher deleted those. IT's working on it, but those messages may be gone for good." Jake sawed through a corner of his enchilada and dumped some salsa on the bite. "We may have to create a fake account and troll for comments. Can't be too obvious, though, and give it away."

"Sounds like a good plan." Kyra kept her lips sealed on the subject for the rest of the lunch and just savored Jake's company.

They hadn't been a couple for long and obstacles kept popping up in their path, but the fact that they both still seemed committed to working through those obstacles made her heart sing with hope. She hadn't let a man this far into her life...ever. She hadn't scared Jake off, yet.

When he finished his enchiladas, Jake moved his plate to the side and patted the booth seat next to him. "Slide on over here. I hope you weren't kidding about those stolen kisses—stolen spicy kisses."

And like a couple of schoolkids, they smooched their way through the rest of the lunch.

They returned to the station late, and Villareal gave Kyra the bad news that only one of the witnesses from the lake at Echo Park remembered seeing Sean's car there...but nothing else.

"We'll keep searching, though, and let me know if you get any more text messages." Villareal rapped on her desk. "I've already informed Detectives McAllister and Crouch, so the task force is up-to-date."

"Thanks, Manny. I appreciate your keeping me informed."

Kyra left without again seeing Jake, who'd been roped into reviewing footage from the last dump site. She couldn't face a third degree from Quinn, so she headed straight home for a jog on the beach bike path and leftovers for dinner.

She let Spot into her apartment to avoid the light smattering of rain that had come in from the north. Then she poured herself a glass of red wine and kicked back in her recliner with her laptop resting on her thighs.

She hadn't checked Websleuths for a while, and the site didn't disappoint. The admins had already established a new message board for the murder of Sean Hughes. Jake hadn't told her that, and he must've seen it having spent all morning on the website.

She checked back in with the case of the missing
Alabama student and posted a few theories and questions of her own. A few minutes after her posts, her
private message notification popped up.

Toby Dog had queried her again about joining the
IRL group, which stood for in real life. This time she
answered that school and work kept her too busy to
get involved.

They messaged back and forth about the Alabama
case, and then Toby Dog sent her a warning that made
her heart pound. She took a sip of wine and read the
message aloud to Spot: "Just don't want to see you
get involved with some weird characters on here."

"Weird characters?" she asked.

He responded that there was a user who had sent
out a few private messages about committing murder and the rules you had to follow to avoid capture.

Kyra stared at the blinking cursor. Rules? Both
Cannon and Fisher had mentioned something about
a rule before they'd died. Her fingers flew over the
keyboard as she asked Toby Dog why she in particular should be concerned about this member.

His answer made her take another swig of wine.
Apparently, this poster had multiple usernames, and
Toby Dog thought she might be the same member
under another name.

She asked him why he'd think that.

When his answer came, she rubbed her eyes and
read it through again.

Because one of the usernames he used was Laprey.

Chapter Ten

Jake finished reading the final report on the CCTV footage on the most recent dump site, just as Fiona put the last of the dishes into the dishwasher.

He snapped his laptop closed and said, "That wasn't so bad, was it? And don't pretend your mother doesn't make you do chores at home. She already filled me in."

"Was that when she was telling you to keep your new girlfriend away from me?" Fiona threw him a look that was half challenging, half fearful.

His hands clenched, and then he took a deep breath through his nose, blowing it out through barely parted lips. "Does Kyra's past really worry you? She killed a man in self-defense. She killed a man, not only to protect herself but a younger child in the home. Yeah, she's no stranger to violence, but some kids don't have it made—like you do."

Fiona had the self-awareness to look ashamed, or at least she'd dropped her bold gaze. "Actually, Mom's the one who freaked out when I told her. I think it's kind of badass."

"Language, please." Jake folded his arms. "So, you *are* the one who told your mother. I thought it unlikely that she was reading the *LA Confidential* blog up in Monterey."

"Well, you're both always telling me not to keep secrets."

Should he confront her with the Jazzy Noir page and wipe the smug smile off her face? His personal cell phone rang, saving him from making a decision. Even better, the call was from Kyra.

"What's up?"

Fiona made a show of opening the refrigerator and studying its contents.

"I made a discovery tonight." Kyra sounded breathless, which made his pulse jump.

"What kind of discovery?"

"I think Laprey has been on Websleuths, and I think he may have been in touch with the copycats."

The blood rushed to his head, and he squeezed the phone. "How do you know this?"

"Because I've been scrolling through Websleuths myself."

He should've known, but a thrumming excitement replaced any irritation he felt. "Start from the beginning. Don't leave anything out."

He scribbled notes on a pad of paper as Kyra told him about using the name Laprey to create an account on Websleuths and the private messages she'd been exchanging with people on the site.

When she finished, he asked, "What kind of rules was this person spouting off?"

"He didn't say, exactly. The whole thing spooked him, and he didn't want anything to do with that poster."

"Did he tell you some of the other names this user had?"

"LA Guy was one of them. Card Sharp was another. Get it? Card Sharp."

Jake got it. "We need to question this Toby Dog, Kyra, but don't tell him anything. I don't want to scare him off. He may not want to get involved. I'm going to have IT trace him and those usernames he mentioned. When we get in touch with Toby Dog, I want it to be a surprise."

"Jake, I'm sorry I went behind your back on Websleuths and then didn't tell you."

"I thought we were past all that. You still don't feel as if you can trust me?" His gaze shifted to Fiona, huddled over her phone, and he got up and sauntered to his window on the city.

"I absolutely trust you. You know it's my nature to be secretive. To hold back one little bit of myself." She took a drink of something. "It's a process."

If he couldn't share her with his daughter, Kyra had every right to hold back. "I get it, but I'm glad you understand the importance of sharing those secrets when it could be someone's life or death…maybe even yours."

"I may have messed things up, though. If Laprey is on Websleuths and he's had contact with the copycats, he will have seen my username. He'll understand that we must know about that site." She smacked something, and he hoped it was a table and not herself. "I could've just ruined that option for you."

"Don't worry about that now. I'm going to get Brandon working on tracing the IP address of Toby Dog tomorrow morning, so we can find out what he knows. In the meantime, stay off the site. Don't delete your account, just in case the other Laprey gets the brilliant idea of contacting you."

"I promise. I'm done with Websleuths."

"Unless Laprey messages you. Then you're going to respond to him."

"If he does that, I'll contact you first."

Jake stared into the night and traced a finger across the glass. "More and more, I'm beginning to believe Laprey is connected to the copycats. I don't know if he's egging them on or if he's also a killer. He knows about you, and that's some kind of sick side game for him."

"I don't like being someone's sick side game, but I may have destroyed any chance to nail Laprey by diving in without thinking."

"Don't keep beating yourself up. We'll get him." He ended the call and tapped his phone against his chin.

Fiona cleared her throat behind him. "Can I have the rest of this ice cream?"

"Go for it."

"Everything okay?"

He turned toward his daughter as she reached into the freezer. Did she care? She typically didn't ask him about his work, and Tess wouldn't be too happy if he answered truthfully. "All good."

"Can I stay with Lyric this weekend?" She spooned some ice cream directly from the carton into her mouth.

Jake sank down in front of his laptop again, ready to do more digging into Websleuths. "All weekend?"

Waving the spoon in the air, she said, "I'd go out there Friday after school and come back on Sunday."

"I'll call Mrs. Becker first."

"She already said it's okay."

"Then everything should check out."

"Looks like you're gonna work some more, so I'll get that last set of algebra problems done." She grabbed the laptop from the coffee table and swept upstairs.

Jake stared after her. Fiona must've been desperate to get away from her mother, or the whole thing was a ruse so she could visit Lyric. She sure hadn't come here for him.

Maybe like a high school kid with his parents out of town, he could sneak a few nights with Kyra. It wouldn't hurt to keep an eye on Kyra right now. Laprey's actions marked him as more than a merry prankster, and with every passing day he was getting closer to Kyra…and more threatening.

THE FOLLOWING DAY, Jake and Kyra crowded into Brandon Nguyen's small office on the first floor of the station, where Brandon had four different monitors running, one of them displaying the Websleuths site.

Sitting next to Brandon, Kyra jabbed her finger at the screen. "That's him—Toby Dog. He's the one who warned me about this other user."

"As I already established a rapport with the admins of this site, it shouldn't be a problem for me to get the details on Toby Dog and track him down through his IP address. If they want a warrant...?" Brandon cranked his head over his shoulder and raised his eyebrows at Jake.

"Let me know. I'll be in and out of the station, so text or call when you have something." As Jake squeezed out of the office, his phone rang and he plunged his hand in his pocket to grab it.

"J-Mac, it's LaTonya in Dispatch. Call just came in for a dead body out in Topanga Canyon." She lowered her voice. "I can tell you right now from the details I heard, it's Copycat Three."

"I appreciate the heads-up, LaTonya. I'm sure it's going to be maximum activity up at the task force." Jake pocketed the phone and told a waiting Kyra and Brandon the news. "Another body."

"Just gave me even more incentive." Brandon swiveled his chair back to one of his computers and started tapping the keyboard.

As they walked upstairs, Kyra said, "I'm going to follow you and Billy over. Can you text me the location when you get it?"

"I will."

Ten minutes later, Jake and Billy were hauling tail to the dump site in Topanga. Jake didn't bother checking the rearview mirror to see if Kyra was following them—she had as much riding on this case as anyone.

When they arrived, the LA County Sheriff's Department had cordoned off the area, and two deputies were talking to a couple with a dog prancing around their feet.

Jake nodded toward the scene. "Couple out hiking with their dog, and the dog made a gruesome discovery."

Billy had the door open before Jake even stopped the vehicle. He called back over his shoulder. "Let's see if he took the bait from *LA Confidential*."

Jake parked the car and strode up to the deputy and the couple.

Deputy Vega introduced himself and the couple. "This is Timothy Beauchamp and Skye Duncan. They were hiking and the dog found the body."

The young, bearded man slung his arm around the woman and said, "We didn't see a thing from the trail, although I guess if we were looking that way we could've. Gus, our dog, took off running. We thought he'd spotted a squirrel or something, but when he wouldn't come back to us, I went over to take a look. Sh-she had…"

Skye crossed her arms and hunched her shoulders. "We had to drag him away by the collar and snap on his leash. I—I hope Gus didn't disturb the crime scene or anything."

"Why do you say that?" Jake looked past their shoulders at Billy, who was coming out of the trees, shaking his head.

Timothy said, "He had something in his mouth when I grabbed him. Maybe it was just some trash or something."

Jake studied the ground at their feet, the dog still panting and straining against his leash. Jake scratched Gus behind the ears. "Did he drop it or eat it?"

"He must've dropped it." Timothy turned in a circle, his hiking books crunching the twigs and leaves on the ground. "I don't see it, and I don't think he'd eat anything that wasn't food."

"Don't worry about it. We'll have a look." Jake turned to the deputy. "Can you finish taking their statement? And I need you two to stick around."

Skye tugged at Gus's leash. "Can we walk away from here a little so Gus will settle down?"

"Sure." Jake patted the dog's head. "Good boy, Gus."

He tromped down the trail in his wingtips to meet Billy, stationed beneath a big maple tree, its leaves just starting to change color. "What's wrong? Not Copycat Three?"

"Oh, it's our boy, all right—queen of clubs in the mouth, severed finger and missing underwear."

"Then why the shaking head?"

"He didn't leave a communication for you. He didn't take the bait."

Jake glanced back toward Gus, who was barking as Skye led him down the trail. "Maybe he did. The dog got to the body first and took something away from the scene."

"Just great." Billy pointed up toward a ridge.

"There's a road up there. I think he dumped the body from up there, climbed down and set the scene. No way he hiked in here with a body slung over his shoulder."

"Good call. We'll take a look at the road for any evidence. Strangulation?"

"Looks like it to me. I'm wondering how he's getting these women to come with him. No sign of drugging like with Jordy." Billy brushed a twig from the shoulder of his jacket with his gloved hand.

"The cars of Juliana and Carmella were found near clubs in Hollywood, unfortunately in lots with no cameras. He must be intercepting them outside the clubs. Both bodies showed high levels of alcohol. He's taking advantage of their inebriation, probably not hard for him to maneuver them into his car. Strangles them there and dumps them." Jake squeezed past Billy toward the body. "We need to get a few people at those clubs."

Jake yanked a pair of gloves from his pocket and pulled them on, flexing his fingers. He crouched beside the body of the young woman, her long brown hair neatly arranged over her shoulders. Textbook Copycat Three.

He murmured, "How'd he get you to go with him?"

"J-Mac! I got it!"

Jake looked over his shoulder to take in Billy waving something white above his head. He rose to his feet and approached his giddy partner.

Billy held out the crumpled, sticky envelope with Jake's name on it. "The dog must've had it in his mouth. There's a little drool and a little tear, but he didn't rip it open or destroy it."

Jake pinched the envelope between two gloved fingers, his breath hitching in his throat. He flipped open the unsealed envelope and slid one finger inside to retrieve the single sheet of paper with the same block letters in ballpoint pen.

He read it aloud to Billy. "'I'm more than a copycat and you're'—spelled Y-O-U-R—'going to find out how much more. I have my own rules.'"

Billy snorted. "At least we know not to look for a grammar stickler. Guess you touched a nerve naming him Copycat Three."

Jake tapped the edge of the envelope against his palm. "There's that notion of rules again. The other two killers mentioned something about rules. Cannon was frantic about breaking rule number four. They're definitely connected by something...or someone."

"I hope Copycat Three *does* start following his own rules, because the rules they've all been following so far have allowed them to kill several women— and that's gotta stop." Billy whipped a plastic bag from his pocket and held it open for Jake to drop the note inside.

That was the last minute the two partners had to themselves as hordes of CSI personnel descended on the site. Jake conferred with the techs before setting them loose on the crime scene to collect, photograph and bag the evidence.

Jake wandered back to the trail, which was clogged with more people, including lookie-loos and the press.

His gaze tracked right to Kyra, her head together with Megan Wright's from KTOP, her cameraman in tow. Kyra had probably given Megan the go-ahead, but the press was going to find out, anyway. The news station had people dedicated to listening to the radio calls of law enforcement.

When Kyra saw him, he lifted his hand and pointed to his car. She gave Megan a quick word and made her way up the trail to meet him.

He leaned against his vehicle, peeling off his gloves. "LaTonya was correct. It's Copycat Three."

"No ID on the body?"

"None, but they'll fingerprint her, and Billy will go through the sad task of reviewing any missing women. It won't be long before they identify her." He shoved the gloves in his pocket. "He left me a note."

Kyra's shoulders sagged as if she'd been holding her breath. "What did he say this time? Was he mad?"

"Lashed out. Said he was more than a copycat and he'd show me." Jake scratched his chin. "Mentioned rules."

"Rules? Again?" Kyra grabbed the strap of her purse and sucked in her bottom lip. "They're all following rules from someone. They're following rules from Laprey. They must be. It's all originating from that website."

"It's crazy, but if Copycat Three is ready to go off on his own, maybe that will give us more opportunity to stop him. Think about it. Jordy Lee Cannon broke a rule by knowing his victims, and Fisher left a fingerprint on that tape. If Copycat Three wants to forge out on his own, let him."

"Forge out from whom or what? It has to be Laprey directing these guys, but why?"

"To create an army of serial killers." He touched her arm. "I'm going to talk to the couple who called in the body and touch base with the CSIs."

"I'll head back to station. Oh, and I got a text from Quinn. He wants to see us tonight. Can you make it, or do you need to be with Fiona?"

"Fiona's going to her friend's place after school, which reminds me. I need to call the mom." Jake pulled on another pair of gloves to ready himself for the crime scene. "Did Quinn text you before or after he heard about this third murder?"

"It was before, so I'm sure he's even more eager now to see us."

"So am I."

KYRA DROVE TO the station with a million questions in her head. Who was giving these killers their marching orders? Was it someone too afraid to do the killing himself? Did he get off on the power while he protected himself? There would have to be some crime the police could charge him with. You couldn't just run around and encourage people to commit murder, give them advice, egg them on.

How would this mastermind know what rules to follow unless he had committed murder himself? Had he already committed murder? If Laprey was the one behind these killers, he most likely murdered

Yolanda, the homeless woman, and Sean. He *was* a killer.

When she got back to the Northeast Division, she had emails waiting for her from Juliana French's mother and more support from her former clients. If only Jake's ex-wife believed she was some kind of hero instead of some undesirable to be kept away from her daughter.

Kyra kept an eye out for the surge of activity that would indicate members of the task force had returned from the crime scene. They'd go through all the familiar steps—trying to identify the murder victim, locating her car, her home, her friends, her family. Jordy Cannon had been a fool to break that rule about knowing the victim. Usually murder victims did know their killers, and once law enforcement cast a wide enough net, they usually caught their man… or woman.

Eventually people started coming in from the field, looks of hardened determination on their faces. Billy always got the job of ID'ing the victim. He had insisted on it ever since his own sister disappeared. It had become a compulsion for him.

When Billy walked into the task force room, he didn't look left or right on his way to his desk. The task would absorb him for hours until he got a break.

Jake followed closely on Billy's heels, talking to three different people and trying to text on his phone. She knew Jake would want to craft another response to Copycat Three, and she'd already started working on it in her head.

They'd want to challenge Copycat Three to break more rules while stoking his belief that he'd outgrown his mentor, whoever that was. They had to walk a fine line between taunting him and encouraging him to commit more murders. But, honestly, the guy didn't need encouragement. The urge had gotten in his blood.

As the day wound down, Kyra texted Jake from across the room, asking if they were still on for Quinn's.

Instead of texting her back, Jake stood up and stretched and then sauntered to her desk.

Wedging a hip on her desk, he said, "I'm good for Quinn's, but I need to go home first. I want to see Fiona before she takes off for Lyric's house and make sure she gets into a car with an actual adult driving and not a teenager. Lyric's older brother is picking her up. Then I'll head down to Venice. Who's cooking?"

"I'll pick up something. Any requests?"

"Whatever Quinn wants." He leaned in close. "We got a break today. When the coroner moved the body, there was a swizzle stick stuck to the victim's back where her shirt was pulled up."

"A swizzle stick? You mean one of those stirrers from a drink?"

"Yeah, kind of unique looking—a rainbow color. We're going to start checking the clubs, starting with Hollywood. It could just be from the victim's location before she got snatched, and if her car's in the same area, it's no mystery. But it seems odd that she'd have something like that stuck to her body from a club where she'd been drinking or dancing."

"You mean, it's more likely that it was in the car that transported her dead body to Topanga?"

"Right." He shrugged. "Unless it was on the ground already and the killer dropped her on top of it."

"That's promising. The footage of the clubs where Juliana and Carmella were before their murders hasn't shown anything yet? Nobody approaching the women? Leaving with them?"

"Nothing like that. Just shows they left alone, which is on my list of don'ts for Fiona when she's old enough to go out to clubs." Jake squeezed his eyes closed and grimaced, as if the thought of Fiona in a club caused him physical pain. "Young women should never leave a bar or club alone—or with a stranger, especially when intoxicated."

"That's the trouble with booze though, isn't it? It makes you do things you normally wouldn't."

"So does hubris." Jake winked. "And I think we have Copycat Three all ginned up on that."

Kyra left before Jake, although she didn't have any clients to see at her Santa Monica office. When she got home, she cleaned up—just in case Jake made an appearance at her apartment after dinner. Then she hopped in the shower, put on some fancy underwear—her hopes still high—and fed Spot.

She ordered and picked up Chinese food on the way to Quinn's place on the Venice Canals. He'd heard the news about the third killing today, and Kyra had told him about Copycat Three's note to Jake.

He'd seemed thoughtful and worried when she'd told him about the reference to rules again. He and Jake could analyze it tonight at dinner. She'd enjoy watching two great detectives bounce ideas off each other.

She parked outside of the walk streets that comprised the neighborhood of Venice lining the canals. Beyond the bridges and canals where Quinn's house was located, Venice could be a rough area. Gentrification had never taken root here, despite the city's proximity to the beach.

Two gangs, Venice 13 and the Venice Shoreline Crips, still had a stranglehold on the drug trade here, but the violence and drive-by shootings that characterized other areas of LA inhabited by gangs didn't manifest by the ocean. Venice still bowed down to its hippie roots, and artists had taken a firm hold of the area along the canals.

She always got a kick out of the tough, old LAPD detective hanging out with the artsy crowd of Venice, but all the neighbors had loved Charlotte and had accepted Quinn as part of the deal.

With the bags of food swinging from her wrists, Kyra knocked on Quinn's red door. At the same time, she called out, "It's Kyra."

His strong voice boomed from the other side of the door, "C'mon in."

Must be a good day. She used her key to let herself in and waved at Quinn coming from the rear of the house. His backyard consisted of a little square where he had installed a patio and a section where he tried to grow some vegetables.

"Don't tell me you're gardening out there." She lifted the bags. "I have everything we need right here."

"Just cleaning up some leaves."

"Don't overdo it." She placed the bags on the counter and picked up a bottle of wine. "Ooh, what's this?"

"I did a little shopping and picked up a bottle for you."

She blew him a kiss. "Thanks, Dad."

Quinn stopped short and almost tripped. "You haven't called me that in a while."

"I haven't, have I?"

"You usually call me Dad when you're feeling… insecure." He narrowed his eyes. "Are you okay? Jake treating you all right?"

Was she feeling insecure? She sensed a storm brewing but couldn't put her finger on its origin. The developments in the Copycat Three case had instilled her with confidence, and they were even getting close to identifying her nemesis, Laprey. She and Jake were on shaky ground due to his ex's objection to her being around Fiona, but Jake was working on that.

"Jake's taking care of his daughter, as he should. We're fine." She pulled a container from the bag and plopped it on the counter. "So fine, in fact, he gave me a detail about the murder scene today."

"Evidence?" Quinn crowded into the kitchen next to her and washed his hands at the sink.

"A swizzle stick from a bar stuck to the victim's back. Could've been a bar she was at...or it could be from the killer or his car."

"That's good news."

Before they could say more, a knock on the door had Kyra patting Quinn on the shoulder and saying, "I'll get that. Not expecting anyone else, are you?"

"I still have a few friends, you know, even though Charlotte was the social butterfly. Ned Verona still drops by."

Captain Castillo's name came to her lips, but she shoved it aside for later as she opened the door to Jake.

He held up a six-pack of beer. "For Quinn—so don't get on his case."

"I guess everyone felt we needed alcohol tonight. Quinn even bought a bottle of wine." She stood on her tiptoes and kissed Jake's jaw. "I told Quinn about the swizzle stick. Any progress on that, yet?"

"We briefed several patrol officers, gave them a picture of the stir stick and told them to keep an eye out at the bars and clubs. No DNA or prints on it, though."

"No ID of the victim?" Quinn had been listening intently from across the room and came forward with his arm outstretched.

The two men shook hands, and Jake said, "Not yet."

Kyra moved into the kitchen and called over her shoulder, "You can get Quinn a beer, but just one."

Quinn growled. "Tyrant."

Kyra smiled to herself. Quinn loved it when she ordered him around. She'd just taken up Charlotte's mantle. "I hope nobody minds if we serve ourselves out of the cartons. I'm trying to save us some dish-washing."

"Fine by me, but don't force me to eat my food with chopsticks or we'll be here all night." Quinn took a seat at the table, cold beer in hand.

"Forks, it is." Kyra handed a stack of plates to Jake and grabbed a handful of silverware. She carried the food to the table and went back for the bottle of wine unopened on the counter. She rummaged in a drawer for a corkscrew and carried the items to the table.

"I'll do that." Jake took the wine and the corkscrew from her and peeled the foil off the top of the bottle. As he twisted the corkscrew into the cork, his phone rang. "That's work. I hope I get to finish my dinner."

He shoved the bottle toward Kyra and picked up his phone. "McAllister."

Kyra clutched the wine bottle by the neck and watched Jake's face.

Noticing her scrutiny, he gave her a thumbs-up. "That's great news and good work, Brandon. Do you think he'll call tonight?"

Quinn took the bottle from her and poured the ruby red liquid into her glass. "Drink."

Jake said, "That works, yeah. Thanks." He ended the call and grabbed his beer for a toast. "Here's to the brains behind IT. Brandon tracked down Toby Dog from Websleuths and sent him a message, explaining the situation. The guy's name is Bret Harrison and he lives in Connecticut. He's anxious to talk to me and will be giving me a call later."

Kyra clinked her glass with the two bottles. "Perfect. I wonder if he was surprised to hear from Brandon."

"If he's a fan of Websleuths, I'm sure he's excited to be part of a real-life investigation. I just hope he's not a poser."

"Poser?" Quinn took a sip of beer and plunged a spoon into the sticky rice.

Jake answered, "Someone who's lying to get in on the action. I'm sure you dealt with plenty of phonies giving you fake information just to be involved."

"We sure did—just never from a website."

As the three of them ate, Jake filled in Quinn about the case. They'd almost finished eating when Jake's phone rang again.

He glanced at the display. "This is Bret. I'm going to put him on speaker."

Jake took a swig of beer and answered the phone. "Detective Jake McAllister, LAPD Homicide."

A voice a lot younger than Kyra expected replied. "Detective McAllister, this is Bret Harrison. I was contacted by Brandon Nguyen about some messages I received on Websleuths."

"I've been expecting your call, Bret. When did you start receiving those messages?"

Jake took Bret through several questions and had him go through all the usernames he believed belonged to the same man.

Bret was thorough, had a good memory and didn't

seem to be playing Jake. Of course, he hadn't saved any of the communications so it was just his word, but with all the usernames IT should be able to track an IP address.

Jake cleared his throat. "What other rules did this guy mention?"

"Standard stuff that you'd expect anyone with any common sense to know about, but he always let stories drop about how he'd done this or that. Claimed he'd murdered a few people in different parts of the country. It was creepy."

"Could be someone bragging, but we'll look into him. Can you remember any of his stories?"

Bret huffed out a breath. "Let's see. He cautioned against taking any personal trophies. He said if you were going to take jewelry, make sure it couldn't be tied directly to the victim. He said he once took someone's unique engraved wedding ring that had a yellow diamond, and for some reason the cops never knew about that. But he panicked and tossed it, anyway."

Quinn's bottle of beer landed on its side, and Kyra pulled the napkin from her lap to soak up the fizzy spill.

Jake finished up his conversation with Bret and cupped the phone in his hand. "Interesting stuff."

Kyra glanced at Quinn's face, drained of color, the lines etched deeply in his flesh, and jumped up from her chair. "What's wrong? Are you all right?"

He shifted his blue eyes to hers, and she'd never seen such fear reflected there, not even on the day Charlotte got her cancer diagnosis.

"Quinn?" Jake pushed back from the table.

Quinn closed his eyes and said, "He's back. The Player is back."

Chapter Eleven

Kyra swayed and gripped the back of Quinn's chair. The call had upset him. She and Jake should stop making him relive his one professional failure.

"What makes you say that, Quinn?" Jake narrowed his eyes. "What part of Bret's narration brought you to that conclusion?"

Kyra's heart slammed against her chest. Jake was taking Quinn seriously. Her greatest fear was materializing before her eyes, and Jake was asking rational questions. She felt like screaming.

Quinn opened his eyes slowly, lashes fluttering as if coming out of a trance. "It was what he said about the engraved wedding ring with the yellow diamond."

"But you said The Player never took any trophies except for the severed finger." Her high-pitched voice sounded as if it belonged to someone else, some hysterical person in a melodrama.

Jake must've heard the tone, too. He circled the table and put a hand on her back. "Sit down, Kyra. Have some wine."

With a little nudge from Jake, she plopped down

in her chair and grabbed her wineglass by the stem, her grip practically snapping it off. She took a gulp, hardly tasting the wine as it ran down her throat.

Reaching over and cinching her wrist with his gnarled fingers, Quinn said, "He never did take any other trophies. That's why I was never sure about the ring."

Jake had dragged the chair at the end of the table around to Quinn and now sat next to him, elbows braced on his knees. "The engraved wedding ring?"

"That's right." Quinn released Kyra's wrist and patted her hand. "One of the victims, Delia Hopkins, had a slight indentation on her left ring finger. I naturally assumed it had been a wedding ring, although there were no tan lines and the indentation was very faint."

Jake asked, "Did her family report the ring missing?"

"That's the thing." Quinn scratched his chin. "Delia was divorced, and her ex-husband reported that she'd tossed the ring in the ocean. Nobody at her office ever reported seeing her wear a ring on that finger after her divorce."

"And the description of that wedding ring?"

Quinn locked eyes with Jake, his mouth grim. "The ex-husband described it as a yellow diamond with an engraving. Nobody—and I mean nobody—today would know about that ring. We didn't put it in the reports as missing because the family claimed she didn't have it at the time of her murder."

Blowing out a long breath, Jake glanced at Kyra.

"That's it. Laprey is The Player, and The Player is the one encouraging and guiding these copycats, living vicariously through the murders he's no longer willing or able to commit."

"That means The Player, the man who murdered my mother twenty years ago knows who I am, where I live, where I work, what I drive." Kyra knotted her fingers in front of her and whispered, "What kind of game is he playing?"

Quinn covered his eyes with a slightly trembling hand. "I'm sorry. I never should've confirmed this to you, Kyra. I could still be wrong. Maybe this Laprey is related to The Player. Maybe The Player is dead, as we expected."

"You don't believe that, Quinn—not anymore." She massaged her temples. "I think in the back of my mind I always suspected he was out there watching me, responsible for these…pranks since the copycats started. Do you think he's doing the same thing with the family members of his other victims? Why would I be special among all those people? My mother wasn't even his first or his last victim."

Quinn had a ready answer. "It's because you're involved with the current cases. I kept in touch with a few of the families over the years. Some of them don't even live in LA anymore. You're right in the heart of it. You're on the task force. Anyone could find that out—and he did. Right, Jake?"

Jake nodded, and a muscle twitched at the corner of his mouth. "The Player must've been tracking Kyra before the task force, though. He may have known her as Marilyn Lake, but to know she'd changed her name to Kyra Chase he must've been looking into her life before he launched his squad of killers."

The shock Kyra had been trying to keep at bay seized her. Her leg bounced beneath the table and she clenched her teeth to keep them from chattering.

Quinn scowled at Jake. "Maybe not. *You* found out who she was."

"I'm a detective with resources at my fingertips. Look—" Jake leaned forward and gripped Quinn's shoulder "—I know you're trying to protect Kyra, but she needs to face the truth to deal with it."

Had she come across as that strong to Jake? Why in the world did he think she could handle the knowledge that the man who'd murdered her mother had been keeping tabs on her for twenty years and was now the same person directing a cadre of killers?

She took another slug of wine and dashed at the dribble it left on her chin. "Jake's right. This is also good news for catching Copycat Three. Bring. It. On."

Jake raised an eyebrow at her and continued talking to Quinn. "The Player has been on this Websleuths site. He's shown his hand. We can find him just like we found Bret Harrison. Our IT guy, Brandon is working on it, as we speak. We're gonna nail him, Quinn. Your nightmare's over."

Quinn aimed a shaky smile at Kyra. "I just want Mimi's nightmare to be over."

Kyra left Quinn and Jake to hash through the implications of The Player being the person behind the copycat killers. She'd had enough for one night. She robotically cleaned Quinn's kitchen and put away the leftover food, wondering if she'd ever feel safe again.

As the night wound down and the two detectives got hoarse from talking, Kyra tipped another few mouthfuls of wine in her glass and sat cross-legged on the floor. "Did you figure out how you're gonna catch him, yet?"

"We're working on it." Jake pointed to her glass. "If you're planning to knock that back, you'd better call an Uber to pick you up. Can't allow you on the road, ma'am."

Meeting his gaze over the rim of the glass, she gulped down half of it. "Looks like I'm leaving my car in Venice."

Jake stood up and stretched, his hands practically touching the ceiling. "We're going to call it a night, Quinn. I'm glad you were listening when I got the call from Bret. I always had a niggling suspicion about Laprey and the connection between these killers."

"Twenty-twenty hindsight and all that." Quinn eased up from his chair. "But I was puzzled from the get-go why the killer was taking two trophies. In addition to the severed finger, Cannon took a piece of jewelry. Fisher took a lock of hair, and now Copycat Three takes their underwear."

"What do you mean?" Maybe her brain was fuzzy from the wine, and as she struggled to her feet clutching her wineglass Quinn strode over to help her to her feet.

Quinn's blue eyes sharpened. "The killers took

one trophy for themselves…and the severed finger for The Player."

Ten minutes later, Kyra sat in the passenger seat of Jake's muscle car, shaking from the V-8 engine rumbling beneath her—or from the evening's revelations.

"Are you okay?" Jake ran a hand down her thigh. "I hope you know you're not spending the night alone. I saw Fiona safely off to Lyric's, so I don't have to go home tonight."

"That's tonight. What about all the other nights?" Kyra hugged herself and leaned her head against the window.

"If you're scared, you're staying with me and Fiona. That's it. Fiona's not a child. She knows her mother cheated on me with her law partner and then married him. If she can handle that, she can handle her dad having his girlfriend spend the night."

"And your ex?"

Jake swung the car onto Lincoln Boulevard and gunned it. "I can handle Tess."

"Tess has an even stronger point now, Jake, even though she doesn't know it. Danger is going to follow me like a heat-seeking missile. I don't want your daughter in my orbit. Think about it. My foster brother, Matt… Yolanda, the homeless woman I was trying to question… Sean Hughes. They're all dead."

"You're not responsible for any of that. He is."

She stroked his cheek. "I'll welcome your company at my place tonight and maybe even tomorrow, but when Fiona returns to your house, I won't be there."

"Then first thing tomorrow, I'm installing one of

those camera doorbells at your place, and we can hook up a system in your carport and around the back in the alley by your bedroom window. You need security at your apartment, whether you're there or not. We can sync it all with your phone. I can spring for an alarm system, too." He poked at her purse with her gun stashed in the side pocket. "You sleep with that in your bedroom?"

"I have been, ever since he left that first playing card by the trash bin."

"That's my girl."

He found a place to park on the street and grabbed her hand as they strolled to the apartment building. When they walked inside her place, Jake did a quick check of all the windows and her sliding door to the little patio where she kept a hearty cactus and a few hanging flowerpots.

"You have good security on those windows and the door, but anyone can break a window and you might not even notice it when you first come in."

"You'll get no argument from me if you want to outfit my place like Fort Knox." She dropped her purse on the low wall that separated the short entrance hall from the kitchen. "Coffee, water, tea?"

"I'll take some water. Is Spot around?"

"You're getting fond of that mangy cat, aren't you?"

"I always had pets, mostly dogs, until my old Lab died a few years ago. I didn't get another dog because my work hours are too crazy. I'd have to hire a companion for him, and then what's the point?"

"That's why Spot is the perfect pet." She stuck a

mug of water in the microwave to boil and handed
Jake a glass of water. "Crazy that The Player would
post that stuff on a message board."

"He probably didn't think anyone with any knowledge would be perusing those messages. Anyone can
brag on there. Bret told us he thought the guy was full
of it. Others have made outrageous claims just to get
a reaction from people. The red flags waved for Bret
when he saw your username and thought you were another iteration of the person trolling for a following."

When the microwave buzzer went off, Jake held
up his hand. "Sit down. I'll get your tea. Is that wine
gonna give you a headache? Do you want an aspirin?"

"I ate enough Chinese food before Quinn's bombshell to counter the effects of the alcohol. I'll be fine,
but I have to admit the wine helped." She sank on the
couch and pulled a pillow into her lap. "In the back of
my mind, I always knew he was out there, but having
Quinn confirm it socked me in the gut."

"Nothing changes." Jake carried a steaming mug
to her, the end of the tea bag fluttering off to the side.
He placed the cup on the coffee table and took the
cushion next to her. "He was always out there, and
now you just had it confirmed."

"He wasn't so careful this time, and you'll get
him." She turned toward him and grabbed his hands.
"Won't you?"

"I promise you that." He slid a hand through her
hair and brought her in for a kiss, the taste of beer
and Szechwan chicken still on his lips. "Is my toothbrush still here?"

"As the only one I have here who could possibly object to your presence is Spot, and he's out on the prowl, your toothbrush is in the holder right next to mine."

"As it should be." He planted another kiss on her mouth. "Drink your tea. I'm going to brush my teeth and warm up your bed."

Folding her hands around the mug, she watched Jake lope off toward her bedroom. How had she gotten so lucky? Bad luck had been dogging her most of her life, and then she'd caught a break with Jake... and Quinn. He and Charlotte had been her guardian angels and Jake had joined their ranks.

She drank half her tea and then put the cup in the sink. She double-checked the locks, retrieved her gun from her purse and shut out the lights. Jake had left ajar the bathroom door that led to the bedroom, and the TV glowed from the room next door.

She poked her head in the room to find Jake installed in her bed, the sheets at his waist exposing his bare chest. He had his phone in his hand and her pulse ticked up.

"Everything okay?"

"I'm texting with Fiona." He held up the phone. "Lyric had a few other girls over for the night, and they just came in from the Jacuzzi."

"Must be nice. Wish I had a Jacuzzi."

"If you hurry up, I'll give you a nice, warm massage." He quirked his eyebrows up and down.

With a thrill tingling through all the right parts of her body, she brushed her teeth quickly and shed her clothing on her way from the bathroom to the bed. When she crawled in beside Jake, he pulled her flush against his body with one arm and pressed a kiss against the side of her head.

She clung to him, running her hand down his bare chest and flattening it against his belly. "It's going to be all right, isn't it?"

He rolled toward her and scooped her close, every line of his torso meeting hers. He smoothed his hands over her derriere and touched his warm lips to her ear. "As long as you're with me, I'll make it all right."

And as he made love to her, his hard body firm against hers, his lips whispering all the words she ever wanted to hear…she believed him.

THE FOLLOWING MORNING, Jake dropped off Kyra at her car, parked in a public lot across from the canals in Venice. He continued on his way to his own place in the Hollywood Hills to shower and change for work. He'd called an emergency meeting of the task force on a Saturday to break the news that they now had evidence The Player was directing the copycats. They planned to keep the press in the dark…for now.

He dialed up Fiona on the way, his call going straight to voice mail. Nine o'clock must be too early for a teenage girl on a Saturday morning after a sleepover.

By the time he got to the station, half the task force had arrived. He'd told Kyra to stay put and start calling around to find out who carried the security systems he'd listed for her before he left.

When he dropped the bombshell at the meeting, the buzz in the room reached epic proportions. He hadn't given Captain Castillo a heads-up first, and Carlos's face across the room had taken on an ashen appearance. It was similar to the way Quinn had looked last night—disbelief, horror and…something else, known only to the people who'd worked that case.

After the meeting, Jake touched base with Brandon, whose job of identifying the creepy poster on Websleuths had taken on a whole new aspect.

The young man smacked his forehead with the heel of his hand. "I can't believe it. Just that one little bit of information about the ring, which he never even mentioned to me, and we've got The Player."

"Not yet." Jake clapped him on the back. "But we're counting on you. Go, do your magic."

"I wish it was magic. One of my guys and I are going to be here this afternoon working on those addresses. I'll let you know when we have something."

Jake approached Captain Castillo, still stationed in the corner at the back of the room wearing a crumpled suit that looked like he'd dragged it out of yesterday's dirty clothes. "Sorry I didn't have time to touch base with you, Captain."

Castillo rubbed his unshaven chin. "Quinn told you about that ring, huh?"

"You knew about it?"

"I knew about Quinn's hunch. I never saw that victim's body. Quinn's partner at the time wasn't convinced the line was from a ring and when the ex and the family told us Delia Hopkins never wore a ring on that finger after the divorce, we gave it up."

Jake braced a hand on the wall next to Castillo. "Delia must've lied to her ex. She'd obviously kept the ring, probably wore it around the house. Maybe she was planning to sell it and didn't want to split the proceeds with the ex, so she pretended she threw it out. The description rings true to you?"

"I didn't remember, but I looked it up this morning before your briefing." Castillo rubbed his eyes. "I'm going to get out of here. My wife wants me to get some decorations down for Halloween."

"Thanks for coming in, sir." As Jake turned, he almost bumped into Trevor Jansen, a detective in Vice, the same detective who'd been outed by Sean Hughes's blog a few months ago. He barely recognized the guy out of his undercover disguise. Jake nodded. "Jansen."

"McAllister, I have some information I think you'll wanna hear."

Jake crooked his finger in the air. "Let's get out of this crush."

He led Jansen to the conference room that housed the task force war room, now devoid of its typical chaos. Jake sat at his desk and kicked out Billy's chair in Jansen's direction.

The detective straddled it and folded his arms on the back. "I saw the swizzle stick that was stuck to the most recent victim's back."

"Yeah?" Jake got a burst of adrenaline that made his head throb.

"I have a pretty good idea where it came from. You know of a strip joint on Hollywood Boulevard called Candy Girls?"

"Neon out front, high-end place as far as strip clubs go?"

Jansen's lips twisted up at one corner. "The owner would call it a *gentlemen's club.*"

"Of course. Aren't they all?" Jake snorted. "You're sure about it?"

"Not saying other clubs can't use the same stir sticks, but I recognize that rainbow design from Candy Girls."

Jake raised his eyebrows. "Frequent visitor?"

"My alter ego TJ Jones was a big fan."

"That's right." Jake snapped his fingers. "Some drug sting went down there. How are they still open?"

"Manager wasn't involved." Jansen lifted a shoulder. "Didn't know anything about it."

"Thanks, Jansen. We'll check it out and get the video footage." As Jansen rose, Jake stopped him. "How's your…friend getting along with Cool Breeze's case?"

"I think she can help Billy find out what happened to his sister. Dina's tenacious." Jansen touched his fingers to his forehead and left the room.

When Jake walked out of the station for his house to change before meeting Kyra, he called Fiona again, and this time she answered. "Did you girls have fun last night?"

"Yeah, it was fun. We're gonna see a movie in

Westwood Village today and go shopping. I'll text you later."

Jake sent a quick text to Fiona's mother with the update and headed home. Almost ninety minutes later, metal toolbox in hand, he pulled up to Kyra's apartment building.

She met him at the door and aimed a toe at a box in her hallway. "Ring camera and two more systems for the carport and the alley."

"Great. I hope your management company doesn't have any objections."

"I doubt they will." She grabbed his sweatshirt and pulled him in for a kiss. "How'd the briefing go?"

"As you'd expect—shock, surprise, excitement. Captain Castillo took it hard, like Quinn."

"This is their chance to nail him, though." She sawed her bottom lip. "There's definitely something going on between those two, some secret they share."

"Maybe it's just the shared misery of a serial killer cold case." Jake dropped the toolbox and nudged it. "I brought these because I figured you wouldn't have the right kinds of tools to install this stuff.

She raised her hand. "Guilty, unless a hammer, rusty screwdriver and a broken pair of pliers will do the trick."

Jake pulled the boxes from the bags, and they borrowed a ladder from one of her neighbors. A few hours later, they sat hunched over Kyra's phone, bringing up all the views from her cameras.

"This is awesome. I can check out my place before I even drive up."

He rubbed a circle on her back. "Does it make you feel safer?"

"Of course."

"Don't get overconfident." He pulled her into his lap, wanting to keep her there forever. "You still have to watch your back. Do you need to go to the gun range? I can get you into the range at Elysian Park." He squeezed her bicep. "Get some practice in."

"I was recently recertified. I think I'm good." She twined her arms around his neck. "Do we get another night together, or is your daughter coming home tonight?"

"Another night." He tugged on a lock of her hair. "How do you feel about strip clubs?"

She widened her blue eyes. "As a patron or a performer?"

"I wish." He tightened his arms around her. "When I was at the station, Jansen stopped me and said Candy Girls in Hollywood uses those rainbow swizzle sticks. I'm going to get eyes on their CCTV, but in the meantime we can check it out on a Saturday night and ask a few questions."

"Wouldn't surprise me one bit if Copycat Three frequented a place like that. Probably thinks he's *the man*," she said, using air quotes. "Don't forget, Jordy visited sex workers after his murders."

"Does that mean you're in?" He held out his fist for a bump and she obliged.

"Hell, I haven't had a good night out at a strip club in forever."

JAKE'S MOUTH WENT dry when Kyra sashayed out of her bedroom in a pair of skintight black leather pants, a flowy white silk blouse and sky-high spiky heels. "That's what you're wearing?"

"Exactly. So, you'd better up your game because this—" she smoothed her hands down the thighs of her pants "—is not going to be seen with jeans and a T-shirt."

"Yes, ma'am. Take some clothes for the morning. We'll drive to my place so I can change, and then later you can spend the night." He wiggled his eyebrows up and down.

"Okay, but one condition. I'll drive my own car to your house."

"Let's dump these boxes in the trash, arm your security system and head out."

Later at his house, Jake shook out a black jacket and slung it over his arm before jogging downstairs. When he hit the bottom step, Kyra turned and shimmied her shoulders.

"That's what I'm talking about. You look hot." She tilted her head to one side, her blond hair fanning out across her shoulder. "Did Billy help you choose that?"

"Give me a little credit for having some taste." He straightened his cuffs. "Doesn't hurt having a partner who's a fashion plate, though."

They drove down the hill and into Hollywood. The pink neon of the Candy Girls sign flashed a welcome, and Jake parked his car in a lot down the street. The club attracted all sorts of people, but the better dressed you were the better chance you had of getting inside.

The bouncer ushered in Kyra and Jake, and before the pumped-up watchdog could feel the gun on his hip beneath his jacket, Jake flashed his badge.

The man's eye twitched. "Official business?"

Jake tucked away his wallet. "Not exactly, and the club's not in any trouble. We're more interested in your patrons."

"I'm Greg. Just let me know if I can help in any way. Buddy, the owner, had a scare recently, and he put out the word that we're supposed to cooperate with you guys at all times."

"We appreciate that, Greg. I'm not here to cause Buddy any trouble. Is he here tonight? I would like to talk to him about getting a look at some of your surveillance tapes."

"He's not, but the manager, Pepper, can help with that. I'll send her over." Greg jerked a stubby thumb over his shoulder. "Would you and the lady like a seat up front?"

Kyra jabbed him in the side with a sharp elbow.

"I think a place in the back will work."

"You got it."

Jake insisted on paying the cover charge although Greg was more than happy to let them in, gratis. Then a scantily clad hostess led them to a table in a dark corner, away from the hootin' and hollerin'.

His gaze wandered to the stage where a woman in a cowboy hat and not much more was slithering around a pole. He tipped his head toward the dancer and whispered to Kyra, "Do you think you could do something like that?"

She slid her hand up his thigh, and his muscles coiled. "Are you planning to install a pole in your bedroom?"

He swallowed. "That could be arranged."

She laughed, a low, throaty sound that made him hard. "Actually, that's becoming quite the exercise trend among suburban housewives."

"Birth rate going up in the suburbs?"

A waitress came to their table. Jake ordered a beer, and Kyra ordered a fruity cocktail.

"That's a first for you. Thought you were a beer and wine girl with the occasional margarita thrown in there for girls' night out."

She tapped his arm. "I'm not likely to get a swizzle stick with beer or wine, am I? Or did you already forget the purpose of this little foray to the dark side?"

"Quick thinking, but you need to give this boy a break. My senses have been overwhelmed from the minute you paraded out of your bedroom in that outfit." He leaned in close, inhaling her sweet scent. "I've had one thing on my mind ever since."

Before their drinks arrived, another woman visited their table. Dressed in black slacks and a white oxford shirt, she straddled a chair and snapped a card in front of Jake. "I'm Pepper, the manager. Greg told me who you were. You want our video footage?"

Jake slid his own card across the table. "Depends on your swizzle sticks."

"Excuse me?"

Their waitress returned, and as she set their drinks in front of them, she said, "Can I get you something, Pepper?"

"No, thanks, Anna." Pepper flicked a finger toward Kyra's drink, indicating the rainbow-colored swizzle stick sporting a cherry and a chunk of pineapple. "Does that meet your approval?"

Kyra dislodged the fruit from the stick and held it up. "This is the one."

Jake asked, "Do you know of any other clubs or bars in the area that use these particular sticks?"

"Couldn't tell you, but they're kind of unique. We order them special from a place in Albuquerque." She waved her hand with its black-tipped nails in the air. "They fit our decor."

"Then, I think we'll want that footage."

"You got it. Can I ask you why?"

"I'm sure you get a lot of regulars here, huh?" Jake's gaze swept the room, and his gut knotted at the thought of some psycho getting his kicks here after killing women.

"Oh, yeah." Pepper ran a hand through her short, red hair. "All kinds."

Kyra stirred her frothy drink. "Anyone get handsy with the women?"

"Oh, yeah."

"We wouldn't mind talking to a few of those women and hearing about their experiences." Jake tapped the side of his beer bottle. "Doesn't have to be tonight. We're here doing a little reconnaissance. We can set up formal interviews later, and I'll send someone over on Monday with dates and times for the footage."

"Hope we have it all for you." Pepper stood up and pocketed Jake's card. "We do tape over."

"Hold off on that for now."

"Will do." Pepper rapped her knuckles on the table. "Drinks on the house?"

"Sorry, can't accept that, but we appreciate the offer...and your cooperation."

When Pepper left the table, Kyra puckered her lips around the straw and took a sip of her drink. "Shouldn't get our hopes up. That stick could've been on the ground when Copycat Three dumped the body. The victim could've had it in her back pocket."

"I realize that, but from hanging around Quinn you must know about a detective's gut feelings."

She patted his belly. "You have it about this?"

"I've had it ever since the coroner placed that swizzle stick in my hand. Felt it even more when Jansen cornered me."

"I trust your instincts." She pointed her straw at the stage. "You don't seem that interested in the entertainment."

He grabbed her hands. "I've got all the woman I need right in front of me."

A dancer sidled up to their table and dipped beside it, her long brown hair swinging over her shoulder. "I'm Barbi. Pepper told me you were a cop interested in our clientele."

Jake asked, "You have a story?"

"A regular. He's a weird dude. Kinda scary."

"Scary how?" Jake kicked out the chair. "Can you sit down for a minute?"

She glanced over her shoulder and perched on the edge of the chair. "When he comes in, he usually requests a lap dance from me. Even in the private rooms, the men aren't supposed to touch us, unless we allow it, but this guy…"

"What does he do, Barbi?" Kyra hunched forward, putting on her therapist's voice, inviting all kinds of confidences.

"He—he likes to put his hands around my throat."

Jake clenched his fists under the table. "Does he hurt you?"

"I have a panic button, and I had to push it once. Security came in and kicked him out."

"That must've been terrifying." Kyra patted the other woman's hand. "He should be banned."

"There's something else. Both times he did it, he called me a different name."

Jake froze for a second. "Was it Juliana or Carmela?"

All the color drained from Barbi's face. "It was actually Jenna, but is that what this is about? Copycat Three?"

A pulse throbbed in Jake's throat. "You're familiar with the killer?"

Barbi placed a hand over her heart. "Not only am I familiar with his crimes, the guy I'm talking about came in here late all hyped up on the same nights as the murders."

Chapter Twelve

Jake almost pounded the table but didn't want to startle an already nervous Barbi. "He was here two nights ago?"

Barbi nodded. "He was here tonight."

Jake gripped the edge of the table. "Is he still here?"

"No, he left about an hour ago."

Jake exchanged a look with Kyra. They'd arrived just about an hour ago. Had he spotted them? "Barbi, can you get away from here and talk to us? I can let Pepper know, if you like."

"I'm sure she'll be cool with it. There's a diner across the street that's open all night. I can meet you over there once I change."

Jake paid the tab, added to the bill to cover the two-drink minimum and left a large tip. After alerting Pepper that they'd need the security footage from tonight ASAP, he steered Kyra out of the club and they crossed the street to the diner.

They nabbed a booth in the back and ordered coffee. As Jake curled a hand around his cup, he said,

"If he was there, he saw us. He already knows what I look like."

"He may not come back to Candy Girls, but surely they know his identity, have his credit card receipts." Kyra poured cream in her decaf coffee. "Still, for all we know, Barbi's weirdo might just be some creep who gets off on threatening women. He wouldn't be the first or the last."

"And a swizzle stick from the club he frequents ends up at a dump site for one of the victims? I can't wait to ID this guy and check his alibis, his phone records, his computer."

Kyra put her hand up and wiggled her fingers. "Barbi just walked in."

The woman who approached their table in jeans, sneakers and a hoodie looked like a college student. She adjusted her glasses and slid into the booth next to Kyra.

Jake said, "Thanks for meeting with us. Coffee?"

"Lottie knows what I like."

Barbi waved to the waitress behind the counter, and she called back. "You want the regular, hon?"

Barbi nodded and gave her a thumbs-up. When she turned her attention back to Jake, she said, "I'm glad you came in. I never called the police because I thought I was overreacting. I didn't want to be laughed at."

"We never laugh at possible tips. We get thousands. It's our job to figure out what's viable. Not yours. How and why did you make the connection between your customer and the murders?"

"I've been following all of the copycat cases. In my line of work, you need to watch your back. For Copycat Three, I noticed his victims all had long, brown hair." She flipped her own long, chocolate-brown locks over her shoulder. "I also know he strangles his victims. This guy, Mike is his name, is strange. He always comments on my hair. When I give him lap dances, he wants my hair over my shoulders, and then he put his hands around my neck twice."

Jake tapped a fingernail against his cup. "So, you checked his appearances against the dates of the three murders?"

"I didn't have to dig that much. I keep a notebook of my lap dances for tax purposes." Barbi shoved aside the silverware as the waitress brought her a vanilla milkshake. "When the third woman was murdered the other day, I noticed the coincidence and it gave me a chill."

"Do you know Mike's last name?" Jake had pulled out his phone to take notes.

"Afraid not. I don't even know if Mike's his real name." She held up a perfectly manicured finger. "And before you ask, he always pays cash. You won't find any bar receipts for him."

"But we will see him on camera."

"For sure. I can identify him for you." She stirred her milkshake with a straw. "How did you tie him to Candy Girls?"

When Kyra opened her mouth, Jake nudged her foot under the table. They'd already told Pepper. They didn't have to announce it to everyone. "We'd rather not say right now."

He questioned Barbi for another half hour. She had her stuff together and would make a great witness if they got that far. After the interview, Jake and Kyra walked Barbi to her car, and then returned to his.

Back behind the wheel, Jake said, "This evening turned out even better than I expected when I saw you in your leather pants."

"The night is still young." She trailed her fingernails along his forearm, and he shivered at the promise.

He started the car and pulled out of the lot. "I am going to have to hit the station again tomorrow. I need to get all this info out and send someone over to collect the video from Candy Girls. Barbi said she's available to view it."

Kyra fluttered her lashes better than any one of those Candy Girls. "I promise not to keep you up too late."

THE FOLLOWING MORNING, Jake left Kyra asleep in his bed as he got on the phone and ruined a few weekends. He didn't know how he was going to let Kyra go back to her own place. Now that they knew The Player was still alive and had his sights set on Kyra, Jake wanted to keep her by his side always.

He put a call in to Fiona and almost dropped the phone when she answered after two rings. "I wasn't sure you'd be up this early."

"Who said we ever went to bed?" He heard giggling in the background.

"Man, you just ruined it. How long are you staying at Lyric's today? Is all your schoolwork done for tomorrow? You have one more week to hit it hard online before I put you on a plane back to your mother's and back to regular school."

"Until I come back for Christmas?"

"Yeah, you're still coming for Christmas. I think you handled yourself well this week. I—I'm proud of you."

"Aw, thanks Dad, and yeah, I'm done with homework until my teachers pile on more tomorrow. I even got some help from Lyric's brother on my algebra this weekend."

Was she piling it on too thick? His hinky meter twanged. "Really?"

"Lyric had some math homework to finish before her mom let the other girls come over, so we worked with Ocean."

"You worked with what?"

"Ocean, he's Lyric's brother."

"Figures." Jake glanced up as Kyra came down the staircase in one of his T-shirts. "I can pick you up this afternoon."

"That's okay. Ocean can give me a ride back. He likes driving down Sunset."

What young man didn't? "All right. Keep me posted. I have some work to do today, but I'm available at any time to pick you up if you change your mind—or if Ocean does."

"Okay. Gotta go. Love you."

The back of his eyes prickled. He didn't hear that from her too often.

"I love—" She'd already hung up and cut off his words. God, he needed to say that more often, too.

Kyra climbed onto the counter stool next to him and yawned. "Is Fiona okay?"

"She's going to hang out with Lyric until this afternoon."

"Lyric? That's a pretty name."

"You don't even wanna know what her brother's name is." He pushed away from the counter and moved toward the stove. "I made eggs, I've got coffee going and I can make some toast."

"Sounds good." She tapped his notes on the counter. "Working hard already?"

"The task force is excited about these new developments." He pounded his chest. "I can feel it in here. We're close."

He didn't tell her about the other feelings he had— the sense of dread that had been hanging over him since they'd found out Laprey was The Player.

Someone had suggested that maybe The Player had given the information about the yellow diamond wedding ring to someone in prison, and that person was the one trolling message boards. Jake didn't believe that. The Player had never told anyone about his crimes before this.

"I hope so." Kyra held her hair back with one hand as she took the plate of eggs from him. "I don't know how long I can stay on high alert."

"Have you checked your security system yet this morning?"

"I've barely opened my eyes. Haven't even looked at my phone, yet." She speared a clump of eggs and waved the fork toward her purse on the floor next to the couch. "I didn't charge my phone last night."

"Hope it's not dead." Jake carried his coffee mug into the living room and retrieved her purse. "You also left your gun in your purse."

She dropped her lids halfway over her eyes and said, "I had other things on my mind last night...and other forms of protection."

"Don't remind me about those other things, or we'll never make it out the door this morning." He swung her purse onto the counter, and she pulled out her phone.

"Still juiced." As she cupped her phone in her hand and scrolled through messages, Jake's work phone rang, the jangling sound that always got his heart pumping when he was in the middle of an investigation.

He glanced at the display before he answered, tapping the speaker function at the same time. "Tell me you nailed the SOB, Billy."

"Not yet, but we ID'd the third victim. Her name is Sydney Walsh. Found her car blocks away from a bar downtown, purse and dead cell phone in the car. He must've snatched her there, like the other two."

"Getting the security footage from the bar and the street?"

"On it. The lot where she parked her car doesn't

have any cameras, but there's a bank across the street. We're going to be looking at their ATM camera. Maybe we can catch something from that."

"Family here?" Jake shifted his gaze to Kyra, who'd dropped her fork.

"I don't think so. Roommate reported her missing. Tell Kyra I'll send her the family contact when I get it. Good work, last night, by the way. Hopefully, Sydney will be Copycat Three's last victim."

"I sent Vickers and Moreno out there to retrieve the video. They'll review it with Barbi this afternoon. I was going to have them grab the footage tomorrow, but once Barbi told us Mike had been there last night I expedited the request."

Billy asked, "What are the chances his name is really Mike?"

"Most likely slim and none, but you never know. He probably didn't think we'd be tracking him back to Candy Girls."

Billy lowered his voice. "How was Candy Girls, anyway? I heard the girls there are first-class hot all the way."

Kyra cleared her throat. "Hi, Billy. It's Kyra."

"Damn, J-Mac. Can't you warn a brother?" He coughed. "Hi, Kyra. I meant to say, I heard there were some fine young women working there."

"There are. One of them just might help you catch a killer."

Jake finished some business with Billy and ended the call.

"Now I have an excuse to go into the station

today." Kyra ate the last of her scrambled eggs. "I'm going to start working on resources for Sydney's family and friends. Is that okay with you? I have to be near the action, Jake."

"I know you do, and it's fine with me. You *are* part of the task force."

"Aren't you glad I brought my own car? Now you can head off to work anytime you like, and nobody will be the wiser."

Jake threw back the rest of his coffee. "Don't kid yourself. Everyone already knows we're sleeping together."

As he turned, Kyra put her hand on his arm. "Is it more than that?"

He pulled her off the stool and whispered against her lips, "It is for me."

An hour later when he arrived at the station without Kyra, Brandon pulled him aside. "Amid all the good news today, I gotta be the one to spoil the party."

Jake tensed. "What is it?"

"Those IP addresses for Laprey and his aliases? All fake."

Jake shook his head. "Fake how?"

"All housed with servers in other countries. He patched and spliced through. Probably why he used so many different usernames and accounts. He moved from server to server."

"That means you can't track him."

"Not through the accounts he used on Websleuths."

"Damn." Jake slammed his fist on his desk. "Can

you keep trying to recover his private communications?"

"I will. I'll get as much data as I can on this guy— who else he messaged on that board, what he communicated. It's not nothing, Detective."

"I know that, Brandon. It allowed us to connect him to the copycat killings and identify him as The Player—the original." Jake studied Brandon as he adjusted his glasses and looked away. "What? What's wrong?"

"I mean, is he really The Player? I heard that's based on some flimsy proof from Roger Quinn, the detective who couldn't solve the case. Some people are saying Quinn is just piggybacking on this to clear his own cold case."

"Is that what they're saying?" Jake squinted and Brandon took a few steps back. "They can believe what they want, but as long as I'm head of this task force, that's the party line. Believe it or not...at your own risk."

"Yes, sir. I mean, I'm not saying I don't. I'm just saying..." Brandon trailed off and swallowed.

"Glad you told me." Jake aimed a finger at Brandon's chest. "Now you're treating him as if he is The Player, right?"

"Absolutely, sir." Brandon retreated from the desk.

Jake rubbed his chin. Did the rest of the task force think he was too tied to Quinn and the old cases? Kyra's mother's case? Hell, what did it matter? They'd stopped the first two copycats and with the information from Barbi, they'd stop the third. And if his instincts proved right, they'd catch The Player, too, and he could hand him on a silver platter to Quinn... and Kyra.

A hushed whisper rippled through the room, and several of the guys crowded at the window.

He looked at Morgan Reppucci, the lone woman in the room "What's going on?"

Morgan rolled her eyes. "They just heard that the dancer from Candy Girls is in the parking lot."

Jake clapped his hands. "What're you guys? Thirteen?"

Morgan said, "That's what I'm saying."

Morgan's partner peeled away from the window and shoved her shoulder. "Don't give me that. When we saw The Rock in that restaurant, you had to wipe the drool from your face."

Jake laughed along with the guys, and Morgan reddened. "That's different."

One of the officers peering outside said, "Never mind. She looks more like a Barbara than a Barbi, anyway."

Luckily for Barbi, she was not headed for the task force war room. Brandon had set up a computer, queuing last night's Candy Girl surveillance video in one of the small conference rooms. Billy was meeting her downstairs and taking her up to the viewing room.

Barbi had requested that Kyra be in the room with them, and Jake approved of that. Kyra had been in the club last night, too. Maybe she'd remember the guy.

Jake tried to keep things in perspective. All they had right now was a swizzle stick on the body from a gentlemen's club where Mike liked to place his hands around the neck of a lap dancer. So far they only had Barbi's word that Mike had been there on the same nights as the murders. But once they had a suspect, they could start looking into him.

Kyra walked into the war room, nodded in his direction and stashed her purse in the bottom drawer of her desk. She pointed at the door and exited again.

He followed her out. He'd have to give her the bad news about The Player's IP addresses, but that could wait. When he caught up to her, he asked, "Everything okay at your place?"

"Everything's fine. I reviewed my security cam, and nobody even came close to my apartment last night or this morning."

"Good. Did you feed Spot?"

"I swear, if you're so worried about that flea-bitten critter, you should take him in at your house."

"That would give Fiona even more reason to come back." They arrived at the conference room where Barbi, her face devoid of makeup, her hair in a braid, sat in front of the computer.

Still a pretty woman, but not what the guys in the other room had expected. "Hi, Barbi. Thanks for coming to the station."

From behind her glasses, her eyes sought Kyra's face, and Kyra smiled and took the seat next to Barbi. "Are you doing okay?"

"Yeah, just want to get this over with. I am so creeped out right now."

Billy reached for the mouse. "It'll be easy."

Jake hovered over Billy's shoulder as Billy clicked the mouse and said, "This is the club's opening last night. Pepper gave us everything."

Jake held out his hand. "Before we start, to be clear, Barbi, you're saying Mike came to the club twice this week, right? The night before we found that body in Topanga Canyon and last night."

"That's right. The first time, he was all excited and pumped-up, last night not so much. He has mood swings like that. When he's down, he usually doesn't request a lap dance."

"Okay, hit it, Detective Crouch."

Billy started the footage, and Barbi hunched forward to peer at the customers coming through the door. Thirty minutes in, she jabbed her finger at the screen. "That's Mike."

They all seemed to expel the same breath, as Billy stopped the video and snapped a picture of the frame showing a big guy with sloping shoulders in a jacket with a motorcycle on the back.

That was the only distinctive thing about him. He'd turned his face away from the camera—as if he knew it was there—and his hair, an indeterminate shade of brown, obscured his profile.

Starting up the video again, Billy said, "Maybe we'll get a better look at him when he reaches his table."

The camera at the entrance didn't include the club itself, and they lost sight of Mike after he paid—with cash—and slipped through the black doors.

Billy noted the time on a piece of paper, clicked

on another folder on the computer's desktop and sped through the video of the area surrounding the stage to a few seconds after Mike walked through the doors.

They got a good look at some of the patrons as they took their seats, ordered drinks and waved at the stage, but none of the footage included Mike.

"I don't see him. He doesn't usually sit at those tables. He's off to this side." She jerked her thumb to the right.

Billy held up his finger. "All is not lost. There's one more view Pepper gave us from over the bar. Maybe he got caught in that."

Jake murmured, "Or maybe he knows where the cameras are stationed and keeps clear."

Billy launched the third camera view and zeroed in on a table Barbi picked out.

"That's his leg. That's all I can tell you." She slumped in her seat. "I'm sorry I couldn't be more helpful."

"You're not done yet." Jake put his hand on Billy's shoulder. "Detective Crouch is going to take you to see our sketch artist. We called her in today. We'll get a composite out there. That'll be a huge help."

Barbi scooted her chair back. "I can definitely do that."

"And if Pepper can get us footage from the night earlier this week, maybe we'll have better luck finding a full view of Mike." Jake leaned in toward Billy as he rose. "Can you find Jansen from Vice and send him in here? I saw him earlier. He used to hang out at Candy Girls when he was undercover."

Billy nodded. "Some guys have it rough."

When they left, Jake said to Kyra, "It's a start."

His personal phone buzzed, and he fished it from his pocket. "Hi, Tess."

"Where's Fiona?"

"She's still at Lyric's house. Lyric's brother is giving her a ride home this afternoon, but I told Fiona to give me a call if she wanted me to pick her up—and I can."

"Jake, it *is* the afternoon. I just texted her and the message didn't show as delivered, so I called her and it rolled right over to voice mail."

Jake's belly fluttered for a second when he glanced at the time on his phone. He hadn't realized they'd spent so much time with Barbi. "Did you call Lyric?"

"I don't have Lyric's phone number, do you?"

"I don't." Jake licked his dry lips. "But I have Mrs. Becker's number. Do you want me to call her?"

"I guess not yet. I'll call and text Fiona a few more times, and you can do the same…when you have time. If we don't get any response by four o'clock, then call Mrs. Becker."

"Okay, I'll text her right now." Jake ended the call and typed a message to Fiona. He tapped the display to send it and watched the little blue text balloon sit there. He twisted his head toward Kyra, busy on her own phone. "I'm going to text you as a test."

"Go right ahead." She held her phone in front of her face. "Everything okay with Fiona?"

"I'm sure it is." He sent the text to Kyra, heard a zipping sound from his phone and watched the Delivered message appear beneath the text. It hadn't done that with the text he'd sent to Fiona.

"Got it." She held up her phone.

"Yeah, I know you did because it says *delivered* beneath it." He switched to Fiona's text and leaned over to show Kyra. "Your text said it was delivered. Hers doesn't. That was what happened the night she traveled from Monterey to LA and turned off her phone."

"Turned off or dead."

"And calls go straight to voice mail."

"Yes."

He hadn't waited for Kyra's answer, tapping Fiona's name on the display. His gut tightened when he heard Fiona's voice. "Not here. *T-T-Y-L.*"

"What does *T-T-Y-L* mean again?"

"It means *talk to you later.*" Her eyebrows knitted over her nose. "Straight to voice mail?"

"Yeah. I'm sure she's okay. She was going to hang out with Lyric this afternoon. If something had happened to the girls, Mrs. Becker would've called by now."

Jansen stuck his head in the room. "Cool Breeze said you wanted to see me."

"We might have a suspect in the Copycat Three case who frequented Candy Girls."

"Got a hit on the stir stick, huh?"

"Thanks to you." Jake gestured with his hand. "Can you have a look at this guy in the video and tell me if you recognize him? It's not very good, but it's all we got. Our witness is with the sketch artist now."

"Sure." Jansen nodded to Kyra.

Jake rubbed his eyes, his gut still knotted. "I'm sorry. Kyra Chase, this is Detective Trevor Jansen, with Vice."

Jansen took Barbi's chair and ran through the portion of the video where Mike entered the club a few times. "Can't help you, but that jacket he's wearing is for posers."

"Huh?" Jake tried to focus.

"He has a jacket with a motorcycle on the back. No hard-core biker is going to wear that. You can cross the bikers off your list of suspects."

"Thanks for your time, Jansen. I'll send you a copy of the sketch when it's ready."

As soon as Jansen stepped out of the room, Jake called Lyric's mother. Her phone went to voice mail, too, but not immediately. "Mrs. Becker, this is Jake McAllister, Fiona's father. Again, thanks for having her over this weekend. Her mother and I are trying to reach her and it seems her phone is turned off. Could you please have her call me? Thanks."

Jake captured his phone between his hands. "If she's pulled another stunt like she did last week, she is going to be in big trouble."

"I'm sure her phone just died—for real this time." Kyra squeezed his biceps. "Maybe you should go home. Everything's under control here. Everyone's doing what they should be doing."

"Go home?" He paced a few steps, dragging his hand through his hair. "You're right. I can't concentrate. I'll check in on the sketch session."

Jake peeked into the room where the sketch artist, Jessica Finch, was working with Barbi.

Jessica gave him a thumbs-up. "We're almost done. She's doing great."

"Great. I have to run so I'm going to hand you off to Detective Crouch. Thanks, Barbi."

Jake practically plowed into Billy in the hallway outside Castillo's office. "Billy, can you handle the sketch when Jessica's done? Make sure Jansen gets a copy. I—I have to get home."

Billy's nostrils flared. "Everything okay with Fiona?"

He must look as panicked as he felt. "She's with a friend, but we can't reach her phone. It's turned off."

"Or the battery died." Kyra pressed a hand against his back.

"Go, go, go. I'm sure she's okay, but you need to be home." He snapped his fingers in the air. "Don't worry about anything. I can handle the sketch and anything else that comes up. It's Sunday. Most of the team will be out of here soon, anyway."

On the way out of the station, with Kyra by his side, Jake tried to text and call Fiona again, with the same results.

Kyra walked with him to his car. "I'm following you home, and I don't even care if Fiona's already there and sees me."

"Do you think she's there?" Jake had a new hope to cling to.

"She might be. Maybe Lyric's brother dropped her

off and she fell asleep. She's probably tired after the weekend she had."

"Maybe you're right."

Jake watched both of his phones on the drive back to his place, jumping every time a text came through. By the time he got home and through the front door, it was four o'clock. He expected a call from Tess at any minute, and he hoped like hell he could tell her their daughter was asleep in her room.

He left the front door open for Kyra and bounded up the stairs, two at a time. He burst into Fiona's room and nearly dropped to his knees when he saw her empty bed.

When his personal phone buzzed, he snatched it from his pocket with an unsteady hand. He took a deep breath before answering. "Mrs. Becker, is Fiona with you? Put her on, please."

"I'm sorry, Mr. McAllister, Fiona isn't with us. She said you were picking her up at The Grove. That was almost two hours ago."

Chapter Thirteen

By the time Kyra reached the bedroom upstairs, Jake was on the phone, pacing, his hand by his side, clenching and unclenching. His gaze wandered past her, unseeing.

"Wait, what are you talking about? I'm here, at home. I didn't pick her up. That wasn't our arrangement, and she never called me."

Kyra balled a fist against her belly. Then she tugged at his sleeve to slow him down.

Jake seemed suddenly aware of her presence and put the phone on speaker just in time for her to hear Mrs. Becker's voice come over the line.

"I'm sorry, Mr. McAllister. That's what Lyric told me."

"Call me Jake. Is Lyric there now? Can I speak to her?"

"She's not home. Sh-she went out to eat with her father."

"Lyric's been home? You've seen her? Talked to her?"

"Yes, yes. Her brother drove her home from The

Grove. She was here for about an hour, and then her father picked her up."

"When do you expect her back? I need to talk to your daughter, Mrs. Becker. Fiona turned off her phone. She hasn't answered our texts or phone calls."

"Oh, my God. I'll get on the phone to her father right now and have him bring her home. You can come right over...and call me Ellie. I'm so sorry, Jake. I didn't know. I shouldn't have allowed the girls to change the plan."

Jake closed his eyes, his nostrils flaring. "It's all right, Ellie. It's not your fault. I'm coming over right now."

"You are a police officer, right? Is there some process you can expedite to find her?"

"I'm going to track down the location of her phone before it went dead...or was turned off."

"Lyric will tell you whatever you need to know... I promise you that."

"Thanks, I'm leaving now."

Jake ended the call and threw his phone at the bed where it bounced once and landed on the floor. "Dammit. Fiona did it again. She lied. But she wouldn't lie this time to get back to her mother's. Then, why?"

"Don't break your phone. You're going to need it." Kyra circled the bed and picked up the phone from the floor. As she pressed it back into Jake's hand, she said, "You're going to have to call Tess."

He grabbed the back of his neck. "I wish I didn't have to tell her anything until I know more."

"Let me drive. You need to get on the phone and

start making calls. How fast can the phone company ping Fiona's cell, and do you need a warrant for that?"

He jogged downstairs and she followed, her hand on the rail so she wouldn't tumble down and plow into him.

"I pay the bill on the phone. I don't need a warrant. I'll have Billy contact the provider, and they'll at least be able to tell me where the phone was when it…went off."

"She must know you're looking for her by now. She may realize what trouble she's in and call you, like last time." Kyra hitched her purse over her shoulder and scrambled for her keys.

As Jake veered toward his car, she took his hand. "My car, remember? Where am I going?"

When they got in the car, Jake reeled off the Beckers' address as he snapped on his seat belt. Then he immediately got on the phone.

Kyra said a silent prayer for Fiona's safety as she half listened to Jake's phone calls. He was calling out all the stops for his daughter.

By the time they reached the Becker residence in Westwood, Jake had spoken to Tess, too, trying to calm and reassure her. Kyra hadn't been listening, but she couldn't block out the frantic voice of Fiona's mother blasting Jake's ear. Parents blamed each other.

Kyra parked on the street in front of a lush green lawn that must've used a lot of water to reach that shade of emerald green in the dry weather they'd been having. A Lexus occupied one side of the driveway, right next to the Tesla.

Jake had the passenger door open before she stopped the car. He strode up to the front door, which swung wide when he hit the first step.

A woman in capris and flip-flops stepped out, her arm extended as if to drag Jake inside. "I'm Ellie Becker. We're having an interesting conversation with Lyric right now."

Kyra joined Jake and stuck out her hand. "I'm Kyra Chase, Jake's friend."

"Come in, both of you. My husband had to leave."

She gestured toward a girl seated cross-legged on a white damask couch that wouldn't survive two minutes under an onslaught from Spot.

The girl sniffled and looked up through a thick fringe of curly hair, her eye makeup creating black rivulets down her face. "I—I'm sorry, but she's okay. She's with Nico."

Jake's body tensed beside hers, and Kyra touched his fingers to ground him. He had a frightened teenager in front of him, not a suspect.

He worked his jaw for a few seconds and managed to form some words in a reasonable tone. "Who's Nico, Lyric?"

"He's Fiona's boyfriend."

Jake twitched, and Kyra tugged at his hand. "Let's sit down and figure this out."

When he sat down stiffly, his shoulder bumping Kyra's, Jake asked, "How does Fiona have a boyfriend down here when she lives in Monterey?"

"She met him online." Lyric's dark brown eyes popped open, as if everyone had online boyfriends.

"He's super cute. He's a surfer and lives in Malibu and he's a junior at Crossroads in Santa Monica."

Sounded too good to be true. Jake must've thought so, too, as the news hadn't relaxed him one bit. His body was so tightly strung it was vibrating.

He barely moved his lips as he asked the next question. "Did you happen to meet this paragon of surfing when he picked up Fiona at The Grove? Were you even at The Grove?"

Nodding vigorously, Lyric said, "Yes, we were at The Grove, but I never got to meet Nico. Ocean, my brother, picked me up before Nico got Fiona."

"You've seen pictures of Nico?" Kyra placed a hand on Jake's forearm, which seemed made of marble...or granite.

"Yes, of course. Fiona wouldn't just meet any random guy that she hadn't seen before." Lyric pushed her curls out of her face and squared her shoulders, as if talking to a couple of fools.

Jake took a deep breath, his chest expanding, giving him a bigger presence that dwarfed the dainty love seat.

Lyric flinched.

"Do you know where Fiona and *Nico* went after The Grove? Do you know what kind of car he drives? Do you know when and where he was going to drop her off? Where online did they meet? Dating site? Gaming? Social media? Message boards?"

That last suggestion gave Kyra a chill, and the rapid-fire questions only confused Lyric. She cast puppy-dog eyes at her mother, but Ellie crossed her arms.

"Answer him, Lyric. How was Fiona communicating with this boy? How many times have I told you not to chat with anyone online that you don't know in person?"

Lyric's mouth dropped open, her ruby-red lipstick smeared across her cheek. "How are you supposed to meet anyone?"

"Answer his questions." Ellie aimed a finger at her daughter that promised hell on earth.

"I don't know any of that other stuff. Wait, he said he had a VW van."

Jake murmured, "Of course, he did. What else do you know?"

"He was supposed to drop her back off at The Grove, but I don't know where they were going. And she met him through Instagram, where else?" She shrugged.

Ellie groaned from across the room.

Kyra asked, "Private messages?"

"Uh-huh." Lyric's pretty face was set in mulish lines. "Direct messaging. Everyone does it."

"Everyone but you, as of now." Ellie retreated to the vast kitchen where she banged around some pots and pans.

Jake's phone buzzed and he answered right away. He paused for a few seconds and then said, "Got it. Yeah, that makes sense. Thanks, we'll start there, pulling footage." He listened. "I'll let you know."

He reported to the rest of them. "Fiona's phone last pinged at The Grove, so no surprise there. It's been off ever since. We can start looking at video as soon as Lyric tells us where Fiona was meeting this guy."

"Oh… Oh, I know that." Lyric wriggled in her seat. "He was supposed to pick her up in front of the movie theaters there, where Ocean got me, but when Ocean and I were driving away I saw her walking on Fairfax and I yelled out the window at her. She said Nico was picking her up at Uncommon Grounds, the coffee place around the corner from The Grove."

Ellie slammed something down in the kitchen. "Are you telling me your brother knew about this scheme?"

"No, I told him it was Fiona's dad picking her up." Lyric started gnawing on a fingernail. "Sorry."

"One more thing, Lyric." Jake managed a smile. "What was Fiona wearing when you last saw her?"

"Oh, I know that, too." Lyric sat up straight and flicked back her hair. "She was wearing a denim skirt with a frayed hem, distressed on one side, a gray T-shirt with red sleeves and the word *honey* on it and white Vans. So cute."

"You were a big help, Lyric." Jake stood up and towered over the girl on the couch. "But you should know that anybody you talk to online can be anyone, tell lies. I hope you're right about Nico being a cute surfer boy, but he could just as well be a thirty-five-year-old predator and Fiona walked right into his trap."

JAKE SLUMPED IN the passenger seat of Kyra's car and dug his thumbs into his temples. "How'd I do in there? I didn't want to scare Lyric or blame her or Ellie."

"You did amazing under the circumstances." Kyra brushed the back of her hand along his cheek, her touch cool and soothing against his flaming skin. He'd been alternating between ice-cold fear and hot rage during that entire interview. How could Fiona be so naive? She should've spent more time in his nitty-gritty world and less in the bubble of Monterey.

"I'm going to have Billy request the footage from Uncommon Grounds. Damn, is that place a magnet for weirdos or what? The first copycat worked and found his victims there, and now some scammer has snatched my daughter from the same place."

"Don't think that way. It's not the same place, anyway. Jordy Cannon's Uncommon Grounds was in West Hollywood. This is a new one at The Grove."

"That makes me feel not one bit better, but thanks for trying. Do you think the Instagram account where she met this guy is the secret one?"

"The Finsta."

"The what?"

"That's what the kids call the second, secret Instagram account. It's a combination of fake and insta. I did a little research the night Fiona showed up on your doorstep."

"I feel so…old." He pulled out his work phone and put in another call to Billy, who was almost as upset about Fiona's disappearance as he was. He instructed him to request the footage for around two o'clock from Uncommon Grounds.

Then he called Tess, who answered on the first ring. She seemed encouraged by the news that Fiona was meeting a boy, and Jake didn't have the heart to set her straight. He wished he could believe Fiona was giggling and stealing kisses with a slightly older high school boy, but his gut and experience had him on a precipice of a black hole of terror.

Kyra tapped the steering wheel to get his attention. "I'm driving straight to Uncommon Grounds at The Grove, right?"

"Yeah, we should get there before Billy, but he'll call ahead so they can be ready for us." He smacked his fist into his other palm. "I should've called her on that secret account. I should've made her show me her private messages."

"Before you go blaming yourself, I'm the one who told you to play dumb on that account. Who knows if you would've discovered anything that way? Seems as if she's been keeping this secret for a while." Kyra sucked in her bottom lip. "You know, it's probably why she came down here, don't you?"

"You mean to meet Nico instead of see me?" Jake clenched his jaw. "Yeah, I know."

When Kyra drove up to the coffeehouse, Jake directed her to park in the small lot next to the building even though cars already filled every slot. "Go ahead and squeeze into that space on the end. I guarantee you will not have to pay any ticket."

She parked and they strode into the coffeehouse, Jake two paces ahead of Kyra. He took a deep breath and slowed his gait. She'd put her life on hold to support him…and he needed her.

Getting his badge ready, Jake approached the counter. "I'm here to see the manager, Melissa Cho."

"One second, please." The young woman at the counter spun around and disappeared into a room off the kitchen. She returned with a woman only slightly older than herself, sporting purple streaks through her straight, black hair.

"I'm Mel Cho. You must be the detective from the LAPD. Can I see some ID?"

Jake flipped his wallet open to expose his badge, and Mel studied it through a pair of chunky-rimmed glasses. "Come around the side. I'll let you into the office. Since your partner called, I've been queuing up the security cam footage from about one forty-five. Do you want me to run it for you?"

"That would be great, thanks." He tipped his head toward Kyra. "My associate will be joining us."

"It'll be a tight squeeze, but we should all fit." She swung open the bottom half of a Dutch door, and Jake waved Kyra through first.

She hadn't been kidding about the size of the office, which boasted one built-in desk, two chairs and a filing cabinet. Jake pulled out the chairs in front of the computer, which had a picture of the front of the shop frozen on the screen. "You two sit down. Mel, you can drive, and I'll hang over your shoulder, if that's okay."

"That's fine by me. I have two camera views up— one for the front of the store and one facing the counter."

Jake said, "Let's go with the one out front first. I doubt they were here for a coffee."

Mel clicked the mouse on the frame, and the figures started moving across the screen. Several minutes had passed by when a girl's bare legs came into view. She had white Vans on her feet.

Jake pointed to the image. "That's her. Can you capture that frame?"

"Just let me know which ones you want, and I'll save them and print them out for you."

"Thanks, Mel. Keep going."

Fiona walked a few more feet, and Jake got a look at the skirt and the red sleeves of her T-shirt from behind. "Save it. Just save every frame with her in it. It looks like she's waiting. She's not going inside."

Kyra tapped her fingers on her knee. "I hope he doesn't just pick her up at the curb. We might see the car, but unless it takes off at just the right angle, we won't get a license plate."

"I don't think anyone can stop on Fairfax on a Sunday afternoon." Mel flicked her fingers at the monitor. "She might walk around back to meet a ride."

Fiona tripped to a stop and turned. Her arms came up and she crossed them over her chest. Her eyes widened and Jake's heart lurched. Even from the grainy footage, he could see fear there, or at least uncertainty.

Kyra must've sensed the same thing, as she shifted in her seat and drew in a breath. "What does she see?"

Jake said grimly, "She probably sees a guy who looks nothing like the cute surfer, Nico."

A larger figure came into the frame, a man with dark hair and a jacket. The hat pulled low on his forehead hid his face. He moved close to Fiona, and Jake clenched his fists.

"Is he touching her? Grabbing her?"

Kyra hunched forward. "I can't see, but he's very close to her."

Mel whistled. "Is he forcing her to go with him? That's what it looks like to me."

"She's going with him." Jake's jaw ached from clenching as he watched this strange man—too big and bulky to be a teen—lead his daughter away.

Mel froze the tape and captured the frame as the couple began to move out of the frame. "We'll get this, and one more as they walk away."

When they turned and Mel stopped the video, a roaring sound rushed through Jake's head and he gripped the back of Mel's chair so he wouldn't fall over. "Zoom in. Zoom in on the back of the guy's jacket."

He didn't need Kyra's cry to confirm the horror before his eyes. The man escorting his daughter away from Uncommon Grounds had a motorcycle on the back of his jacket—just like Copycat Three.

Chapter Fourteen

Kyra covered her mouth with both hands. It couldn't be. Why? How? What did Copycat Three want with Jake's daughter?

Mel twisted her head around to look at Jake. "What's wrong?"

Jake cleared his throat. "That jacket belongs to a very dangerous man. That girl is in big trouble."

The steadiness of his voice amazed Kyra…and worried her a little. "Mel, print all those out. Are there any other cameras that point to your parking lot? Bank nearby? Convenience store?"

"Th-there are a few." Mel clicked the keys on the keyboard, and the printer on the corner of the desk woke up and started spitting out pages.

Jake gathered the printouts and thanked Mel. He walked out of the shop without saying a word to Kyra, who was trying to keep up with him. When he hit the sidewalk, he staggered and placed a hand on the corner of the building. "He has her. Copycat Three has Fiona."

She put her hand over his. "We'll find her. We'll

get her back. You're onto him, and he doesn't even know it. He's gone too far, Jake."

"What does he want with her? Is he using her to get back at me? Does he want ransom or clear sailing out of here?" He pulled Kyra next to him and buried his face in her hair. "I'll give him anything, Kyra. Then I'll kill him."

"Let's get back to the station. Call Billy and tell him. Get the task force on it. You can't do this alone, Jake. Maybe Copycat Three knows you have him in your sights, and this is his way to negotiate an escape plan." She cupped his chin in her palm. "Fiona is not his type. We know that. She's not going to satisfy his urge."

A tremble rolled through Jake's large frame. "It'll satisfy his urge to gut me. He's been planning this for a while. That's what he meant in his note."

When they got back to her car, Jake resumed his phone calls—the first to his partner, Billy.

One thought swam in her head. The Player, the person directing Mike—Copycat Three—wouldn't like this latest development. Mike had gone rogue. The other two serial killers taking orders from The Player had ended their own lives rather than give up their mentor and his secrets. Mike would have to be reminded that The Player would never condone engaging with the police like this—it put him at risk.

When Jake ended one call and before he punched in the next, Kyra touched his arm. "How far did Brandon get with the IP addresses of The Player's aliases on Websleuths?"

He blinked at her for a few seconds. "I'm sorry, Kyra. I never had the chance to tell you that The Player has been using masked IP addresses located all over the world. There's no tracing those back to someone's computer sitting on a desk somewhere."

The news socked her in the gut, but Jake had his own problems right now. "That's bad news, but you'll get him too now that Mike has outed himself in a spectacular way."

"We'll deal with The Player later. If I have an opportunity, and I'm hoping for one, I'll kill Mike without a second thought to nabbing The Player. He just needs to give me one excuse."

"I understand that. Do you think we can communicate with Mike through Fiona's Instagram account? Brandon can probably get us in. It might give Mike pause when he realizes we know about that account."

"That's a good idea. In the meantime, Billy has officers talking to every employee at Candy Girls about Mike—what he drinks, how he pays, who he talks to, what he drives, if they've seen it. I just know it's not a VW van." He slammed his fists against her dashboard. "I can't get over Fiona's face when she saw Mike instead of her teenage dreamboat. She must've been scared. She must've realized she'd made a mistake."

"Fiona is a resourceful girl. Although she showed incredibly poor judgment, she's no dummy. She's going to be fine." Kyra gripped the steering wheel so Jake couldn't see her trembling hands.

When they walked into the station, the task force

war room was buzzing with activity. Billy had called in the troops, and they were here on a Sunday night to support their leader.

She touched Jake on the shoulder before letting him get sucked into the waiting masses. "I'm going to find Brandon."

Jake held up his phone. "Don't bother. I've got a call from an unknown number coming in now."

He put the phone on speaker for the entire room to hear, and the voice proved Jake correct.

"Hey, *J-Mac*, it's the Hollywood Strangler because that's the name I prefer, and I'm calling the shots now. I have something you want."

"Where's my daughter and what do you want?"

Copycat Three choked. He hadn't been expecting Jake to know he'd been the one who'd snatched Fiona.

He recovered quickly. "I'll let you know when I have my list of demands. My *own* rules."

"You mean instead of The Player's rules. We know you've been taking orders from him. You all have. He's not going to like this new development, is he? What rule did you break by kidnapping the daughter of the lead detective on your case? That must be rule numbers five, six, seven and eight."

"Shut up. I'm my own man. He just gave us some tips. I'm my own boss. I don't answer to no one."

"What are your new rules, Mike? What do you want? We can work with you."

"Mike." He snorted. "Who gave you that name? That bitch Barbi? You'd better tell that whore to watch her back. I'll give you my rules when I'm good and ready."

Jake's jaw formed a hard line. "How do I know you haven't harmed her already?"

A rustling noise came over the line and then Fiona's voice. "Daddy? Daddy, I'm so sorry. I'm—"

She didn't get to finish her sentence. Mike returned. "There. She's okay…for now."

Mike ended the call, and it was as if the people in the room who'd been holding their breaths, hanging on to every word, were released from a spell. Talking, movement, phone calls, keyboards—everything came to life at once.

Including Kyra.

She bolted from the room and jogged downstairs to Brandon's small cube. He sat in command over the four computers on his desk, scooting his chair between the keyboards and monitors.

"Brandon, did you hear?"

"I heard." His fingers raced across one keyboard, bringing lines of characters up on one screen. "I just wish I knew who Mike was on Websleuths. Jordy Cannon and Cyrus Fisher never bothered to mask their IP addresses. I doubt Mike did, either."

"There's something else I want you to look at." She wheeled a chair next to his. "Can you get into someone's Instagram and their direct messages if I give you the address?"

"Compared to this?" Brandon spread his hands, encompassing his computers cranking away and spewing out data. "Child's play."

"The account is for a user called Jazzy Noir." She held her breath as Brandon cleared one of his computers and launched Instagram.

He brought up Fiona's secret account, and Kyra scanned it for any new activity. Fiona had posted a few new pictures from LA, nothing too explicit or disturbing—she'd saved that for her private messages.

"Is this it?"

"Yes, can you get into the direct messages?"

"I can if I'm logged in as Jazzy." Brandon's fingers froze. "Wait, is this J-Mac's daughter?"

"It is." She put a finger to her lips. "He's working on something else upstairs. Mike called him on a burner phone, and they're working on tracking down the serial number of the phone and where it was purchased. I told Jake I was going to check Fiona's Finsta. She thinks it's a secret, but Jake has known about it for a while."

"Yeah, I remember those days. I used to have a secret Facebook account that my parents didn't know about." Brandon flushed under her side-eye and got to work.

Lines of numbers and characters raced down the monitor until the display stopped. Brandon crowed, "Got it, baby."

He accessed the application again, bringing up the log-in page. He entered a username and password, and Jazzy Noir's account opened in user mode.

"Oh, my God. You are *the man*. I'm not even going to tell your mother about your secret accounts." She pulled the keyboard toward her. "May I?"

"It's your party. I'll go back to what I was doing before you came in. Let me know if you need any help. I can't believe this guy has J-Mac's daughter. She's just a kid."

Kyra leaned in close to the monitor and clicked the message icon in the upper-right corner of the screen. A list of messages tumbled down the page, the little circles with profile pictures lining up with the names.

She caught her breath when she saw most of the messages from an account featuring a suntanned blond in board shorts with the name of Surfernico. She'd hit the mother lode.

Her heart pounded as she scanned through the messages. Nico/Mike had been filling Fiona's head with everything a girl would want to hear and had roped her in easily. Kyra got to the last message exchanged where they discussed meeting up in LA, but there was nothing about meeting at The Grove. How had they communicated? Hopefully, when Jake got Fiona's phone records, he would be able to see those texts or calls.

Kyra flexed her fingers and took a deep breath. She entered her first message.

Mike, this is Kyra Chase. If you want to make The Player happy, you'll exchange Fiona for me.

She knew enough about this platform to know Mike should be getting an email with a notification that he had a new direct message. She watched the cursor, biting her lip so hard she drew blood. When her phone buzzed, she jumped.

She swept the blood from her lip with her tongue before she answered Jake's call. "Any news?"

"Not yet, but we're doing everything we can. We have a lot of people talking to us about Mike, telling us who he hung out with at the club, maybe even a description of his car."

"Have you gotten Fiona's phone records, yet?"

"Working on it. Where are you?"

"Getting some information from Brandon."

"Anything on Fiona's fake Instagram account, yet?"

Kyra shifted her gaze to Brandon and said, "Not yet. Let me know if you need me, okay? I love you."

Jake paused, taken aback.

Not wanting to put him on the spot, she ended the call.

She whispered to the screen. "C'mon, c'mon."

Ten minutes later, she got her wish. A reply came through on Fiona's direct message. "Who are you?"

She typed back furiously, telling him to check with The Player. Telling Mike that The Player wouldn't be happy that he took a cop's daughter, but he'd be very happy if Mike had Kyra Chase. She made a play for his emotions, suggesting that Fiona wasn't even his type. He wouldn't be punishing the woman he wanted to punish if he killed someone like Fiona.

She held her breath. Had she gone too far?

He made her wait almost twenty minutes, but the

wait was worth it. A pulse danced in her throat as she read his message: I'll take you.

JAKE HAD TWENTY things going on at once, but it helped him keep the panic at bay. They were drawing the net tighter around Mike, but he still hadn't called Jake with any demands. Maybe Mike would wait on those demands until he felt he didn't have a choice. The police still hadn't come knocking on his door, so he had time.

He checked the time. Copycat Three had kidnapped Fiona over six hours ago. What was he doing to his little girl? Jake squeezed his eyes closed and ground his back teeth together. He wanted just ten minutes alone with the guy.

"Jake, Fiona's phone records." Billy shoved a sheaf of papers at him and clapped him on the shoulder. "It's going to be okay, brother. We got you."

Nodding, Jake greedily snatched the papers from Billy's hand and slammed them onto his desk. He pulled up his chair and ran a finger down the last of Fiona's calls and texts. They included calls to Tess and him, Lyric and several texts that looked like they were to friends. He didn't see anything out of the ordinary. How had she been communicating with him?

Must be that fake Instagram account, but if Kyra had found something she would've let him know by now. He grabbed his phone and checked the time. He hadn't heard from Kyra in almost two hours.

Jake stuck Fiona's phone records on Billy's desk. "I'm going to check in on Brandon downstairs. I can't see anything on here from Fiona's phone that points to our guy, but maybe it needs some fresh eyes."

Billy said, "I've got it covered."

Jake jogged downstairs to the IT department and squeezed into Brandon's cubicle. "Where's Kyra?"

"She's, um—" Brandon shoved his glasses up the bridge of his nose "—not sure. She was on the computer for a while, said she had to take a phone call, stepped into the hallway for several minutes and then popped back in here to grab her purse and take off. I thought she was going back upstairs to see you and tell you about Fiona's account."

"Fiona's account?" Jake drew his eyebrows over his nose. "You got in?"

"Yeah, it was easy. I nailed the username and password pretty quickly and handed them off to Kyra."

"Why the hell didn't she tell me that?" Jake pulled out the chair next to Brandon and sat on the edge. "Can you get me into that account?"

"Absolutely." Brandon pulled the keyboard into his lap and accessed the application. Leaning over, he checked another computer monitor and then typed in the log-in information for Fiona's Jazzy Noir account. "There you go."

When he placed the keyboard back on the desk in front of him, Jake started scrolling through the page, his eye twitching at the corner. "Brandon, how do I see direct messages on here?"

"It's that little airplane icon in the upper-right corner."

Jake moved the cursor over the icon, but before he

could click on it, his personal phone rang. He glanced at the unknown caller and answered, "McAllister."

"Daddy? Daddy, I'm so sorry. Please come and get me."

Jake jumped up so fast the chair shot out from beneath him and hit the wall. "Where are you, Fiona?"

"I—I'm not sure. I'm in an alley. He dumped me off in an alley, but he had me blindfolded."

"Are you...all right?"

"I'm okay." She sniffled. "He tied me up. He hit me, but I'm all right, Daddy. He's gone now."

Rage throbbed against his temples. "Are you borrowing someone's phone? Ask them where you are."

"Wait, I see two street signs. I'm at a corner, a busy corner."

"What are the street signs?" She couldn't just ask the owner of the phone?

"It's Selma. Selma and Wilcox."

Relief swept through his body, and he took the first deep breath he'd had in hours. "Sweetie, you're in Hollywood. You're near Sunset. I'm going to send a squad car and an ambulance out to you right now, but I'm on my way. Where is he? Where's... Nico?"

Fiona sobbed. "His name wasn't Nico, Daddy. He was an old man."

"I know that, sweetie. He took you to get back at me. Why'd he let you go?"

"I—I thought you sent her."

A feather of fear brushed the back of his neck. "Sent who?"

"Kyra. Kyra Chase. He let me go...and took her."

Chapter Fifteen

Kyra strained against the zip ties binding her wrists behind her. "She's safe? You left her someplace safe?"

The man in front of her, on the other side of the battered kitchen table, ran a hand through his messy brown hair and crossed his arms over his belly, which hung over the waistband of his jeans. "I dropped her off in an alley with her purse. I left her tied up, but not too tight. Just to give us some time to get away. When she gets loose, she can get to a phone. Glad to get rid of her. She was annoying."

Kyra flattened the smile from her lips. She could only imagine. Fiona had gotten from Monterey to LA by herself; she could figure out how to contact her father or hail down a cop car.

"Who is she, Mike?"

He scowled, his heavy brow hanging over his eyes. "What do you mean? Who is she?"

"The woman with the long, brown hair you keep killing over and over."

He snorted. "You psychologists think you're so smart. Not one of you could ever figure me out. Not one at that third-rate college I went to ever knew what I was capable of. Nobody did."

"Except The Player."

His head shot up, and fear raced through his dark eyes. He tilted his head from side to side, cracking his neck. "Not even he knew. Be careful, he said. Don't engage law enforcement, he said. Don't communicate, he said. I didn't follow that stupid rule, and look where it got me? It got me you."

Kyra locked her jaw for a second to stop the chattering of her teeth. "You told The Player you had me?"

"I did." Mike slammed a fist against the table. "He was worried about that, even after I told him our deal."

Their deal consisted of Kyra staying on video call with him so he could see her leaving the station alone. Nobody would be able to track the phone to her location now because she'd tossed it, along with her purse and weapon, out the car window on the way to their meeting place.

Mike had picked her up on a deserted street corner in Hollywood with Fiona in the car, and Kyra got a quick look at the girl, her face white beneath her blindfold, before he'd shoved Kyra into the car with her and blindfolded and zip-tied her, too. She'd been able to assure Fiona that everything was going to be okay.

Mike had driven around for a while before parking and leading a sobbing Fiona away. Kyra had kept her ears tuned to any sounds of gunfire or violence, but hadn't heard anything ominous.

Fiona'd had no idea where Mike had taken and held her. Mike had turned off Fiona's phone and dumped it. There was no way Jake could trace her back to this small house. The best she could hope for was that the police would locate her car, and maybe Mike's car would show up on CCTV in the area.

"Is he coming here? The Player?" She'd managed to utter his name through parched lips.

"We haven't figured it out yet." Mike stared off into space, and a smile touched his lips. "Her name was Jenna."

"What was she to you?" Kyra straightened in her chair. The more she found out about Mike, the better chance she had of getting away alive.

"College girlfriend, at least I wanted her to be. I played football in college, Division 3 school. I thought that would be enough to score points with her, but she always went for the pretty boys."

Kyra lowered her voice. "Did you hurt Jenna?"

"She had to pay." He rolled his big shoulders.

"You killed her?"

"No." His eyes flashed. "She screamed and some guys from a frat house stopped me. Three on one, that's the only way they could handle me. Kicked my ass and then got me kicked off the football team and out of the school."

"And you've been making her pay ever since." Kyra swallowed. "What do you do with the…panties?"

"I hide them here at home." He puffed out his chest, which consisted of more flab than muscle.

"That's how far I got with Jenna. I got her panties off. Kept 'em, too. I shoved them into my pocket when those frat boys attacked me. Got away with them."

"What do you do with the severed fingers?"

The corner of Mike's mouth curled. "Those are for him."

A shaft of pain pierced her head. "What other rules does The Player have you follow?"

Mike flattened his hands on the table and hunched forward. "What do you know about the rules?"

"The police know more than you think, more than they let on."

He tucked a clump of hair behind his ear and fell back into a chair. "Just the regular stuff. He's not that brilliant. No fingerprints. No DNA—that's why we don't rape them. And then this stupid rule about not taunting law enforcement. What's the point if you can't lord it over them? Lord it over *him*."

"Jake McAllister?"

"Yeah, him. I bet he played quarterback on his football team. Didn't he?"

"I don't think Jake played football. He played water polo. He was a goalie because of his height."

"Water polo?" Mike giggled, an uncomfortable sound coming from a big man. "That's not a man's sport."

"So, maybe McAllister isn't as perfect as you think."

Mike hit the table with his fist, and she jumped. "I don't think he's perfect."

"Did you kill Sean Hughes?"

"Me?" His eyes rounded. "I didn't kill him, but I know who did."

"The Player." Kyra used her legs to scoot her chair forward. "Who is he, Mike?"

Mike bared his teeth when he smiled, which, when coupled with his shaggy hair, gave him a feral appearance. "I guess you're gonna find that out real soon."

ON HIS WAY to meet Fiona, Jake tried Kyra's phone over and over. Just like Fiona's phone before, Kyra's was dead. He'd put in an order to ping Kyra's phone so they could at least get her last location.

How could Kyra have done something so stupid? Why would she trade herself for Fiona? He could've met Mike's demands to get Fiona back, but The Player would have no demands for Kyra's safe return. Jake knew that was the only possible reason Mike would give up Fiona for Kyra—to placate The Player. Kyra had known it, too.

With his heart pounding, Jake pulled up behind the ambulance and jumped out of the car. Fiona hopped off the back of the vehicle and ran into his arms, the silver blanket from the EMTs crunching around her. She sobbed against his chest, and he crushed her like he never wanted to let her go.

"I'm so sorry, Daddy. I didn't know. I never meant for this to happen."

He patted her back. "I know. It's okay. I'm just so happy to have you back and safe. I already called your mother from the car to let her know you were okay. You are, aren't you?"

She pulled away and touched her swollen jaw. "I'm okay. He didn't, you know, do anything to me, but he hit me a few times because I told him what an idiot he was and how he was so much uglier than the picture he used."

Jake's mouth twitched. "Not a great idea to goad a serial killer. D-did you see Kyra?"

"I didn't see her, but I heard her." She covered her eyes with one hand. "Dad, she was so brave. She got into Mike's car, and she told me that everything was going to be okay. That you were all looking for me, and I would be safe now. But, what about her, Dad?"

"We'll find her." He choked. "We'll get her back."

The EMT approached them and said, "She's fine, sir. A little shaken up. We put some ice on her jaw and gave her some ibuprofen for the swelling and pain."

"Thanks. Do you need the thermal blanket back?"

"She can keep that."

A patrol officer approached. "Detective? We're canvassing the area for cameras. We have a description of his car from the club and we'll try to find it on the footage."

"Perfect."

Before he got another word out of his mouth, a second officer approached him. "Sir, we found Ms. Chase's car."

He sucked in a sharp breath. "Anything?"

"Nothing—no purse, no phone, no ID…no blood."

Jake massaged the back of his neck. "Okay, I'll be over in a minute." He turned back to Fiona.

"I'm not sending you back to my place alone. I

think it might be best if I had someone take you to the station. You can wait for me there until I'm done with this scene. I'm so glad to have you back." He pulled her into a hug. "You never told me whose phone you used to call me. Can you point them out? I'd like to thank him or her, personally."

"I didn't use someone else's phone." Fiona looked down at the ground and kicked at a rock with the toe of her shoe.

"I know he didn't give you your phone back. You called me from a number I didn't recognize."

She held up one finger and then dug into her purse. She pulled out a flip phone. "I called you from this phone. I'm sorry. I bought a second phone that you and Mom didn't know about."

A surge of adrenaline flooded his body. "Did Mike know you had this phone?"

Shrugging, she said, "I don't think so. I had my other phone in my hand when he…picked me up. I turned it off myself, but he made me throw it out the window. This other phone was at the bottom of my purse. He didn't ask, and I never told him."

Jake's mouth dropped open. "You had this phone with you the whole time and it was turned on?"

"Well, yeah. Nobody ever uses it to call me—except Nico, who isn't really Nico."

Jake grabbed her shoulders and kissed her on the forehead. "I'd forgive you ten burner phones right now."

KYRA CLEARED HER THROAT. "When is he coming?"

Mike glanced up from his phone, a shock of hair

hanging in his eyes. "I'm not sure. We'll figure it out. I turn you over to him, and I can go on with my plans."

"Are you sure about that?"

"What do you mean?" He wiped the back of his hand across his mouth, smearing the grease left over from the fast-food tacos.

She lifted a stiff shoulder. "Maybe he won't let you continue. You've broken the rules. You've jeopardized yourself and him."

"He doesn't have a say in whether or not I continue. I'm good at this. I haven't gotten caught yet, have I?"

"Haven't you? Once you snatched Detective McAllister's daughter, you entered a whole other realm of being public enemy number one. Do you understand how many people are working to find you now? The Player isn't going to like that."

He bit into his taco and answered with his mouth full of food. "Who cares?"

"I think you should care. Look at what happened to Jordy Cannon. Look at what happened to Cyrus Fisher." She tapped her temple. "Do you have one of those cyanide tablets, too?"

"What if I do?" He dropped the taco, which fell to pieces on his plate right next to a .45. "If you don't shut your mouth, I'll make you take it."

"Where is he?" Kyra caught sight of a light blinking outside behind Mike. Her breath hitched in her throat. Was that The Player now? Would she finally get a look at the man who had murdered her mother?

"He does things in his own way." Mike cranked his head over his shoulder, but the blinking light had stopped. He returned to his taco, picking up chunks of meat and cheese with his fingers and stuffing them into his mouth. "He was happy I brought you in. You were right about that."

As soon as Mike turned back around, she saw the light flash again. Then a red beam lasered into the window. Would Mike see it against the wall behind her? Where had it stopped? Was it aimed at her forehead?

She tentatively rocked her chair to the side while Mike scooped up the rest of the contents of his taco. As his face dipped to his plate, she rocked harder until the chair tipped on its legs. She threw all her weight toward the floor.

On her way down, she saw Mike jump up and grab his gun.

She crashed to the floor, her cheekbone hitting one of the table legs. At the same time, the front door of the house burst open.

"Drop your weapon!"

From her vantage point, she saw Mike's feet pivot toward the other room. He screamed out at the cops, "Did he send you?"

He must've raised his gun because, in an instant, a hail of gunfire erupted in the room and Mike toppled against the blood-spattered wall.

One second later, before Kyra had time to process what had happened, Jake was crouched beside her, snipping the zip ties away and pulling her into his arms. "Are you all right? Did he hurt you?"

She looked into his face, her fingertips lightly resting on his chin. "How'd you know where I was?"

Capturing her hand, he kissed her raw wrists. "We owe it all to my sneaky, rebellious daughter."

Epilogue

"I don't know why he's your favorite person. He doesn't even feed you." She shuffled her feet against Spot to move him away from the door.

"It's male bonding." Jake scratched the cat under his chin to lessen his ire at being denied entry into Kyra's apartment.

Jake placed his hand on the small of her back as they walked to his car, parked on the street. Ever since he'd rescued her from Mike's house, he'd been hovering over her like a mother hen—a hot mother hen.

Mike turned out to be Mitchell Reed, a twenty-six-year-old security guard and former college football player. His story about Jenna had proved to be true. He'd been using his security guard credentials to lure slightly tipsy women into his car as they stumbled out of bars and clubs by themselves.

Whether or not The Player ever had any intention of collecting her from Mitchell's house, they couldn't know for sure. They traced Mitchell's IP address to an account on Websleuths. Like the others, all private messages between him and The Player had been erased. Brandon was never able to track any of The Player's IP addresses to one location.

As Jake opened the passenger door for her, he said, "Are we picking up food for Quinn tonight or did Rose cook something for him?"

"Neither. I'm ordering delivery." When Jake came around and slid behind the steering wheel, she squeezed his forearm. "Fiona get off okay?"

"She did."

"It's a good thing she had that burner phone. She even tricked Mitchell."

"I don't think she was trying to. He tossed her real phone, and she sort of forgot about the other phone at the bottom of her purse. She was accustomed to hiding it in the lining of her bag." Jake shook his head. "How did she get to that point?"

"Don't start blaming yourself. Even Brandon Nguyen told me he had fake social media accounts to trick his parents."

"Brandon?" Jake grinned. "I gotta give him a hard time about that."

"Are you still allowing Fiona back here for Christmas?"

"Are you kidding? She's *demanding* it now because she wants to hang out with you."

Kyra's nose tingled. "The feeling is mutual. Maybe this taught her a lesson, and she'll be better behaved from here on out."

They looked at each other at the same time and said, "Nah."

"She's going to suffer her mother's wrath for a

while. Tess is beating herself up for not monitoring her social media access better." Jake brushed her cheek with his fingertip. "You have a new fan there, too. Tess is so grateful to you for trading yourself for Fiona."

"I knew Mitchell would go for it. These guys have an almost slavish devotion to The Player. Cannon and Fisher literally died for him. Mitchell definitely went rogue in that respect. I don't think he was willing to lose his life for The Player."

"Quinn is so rattled by the idea that The Player is still alive."

"That's why I didn't tell him anything about your abduction until it was all over." Jake drummed his thumbs on the steering wheel. "There are still people on the task force who don't believe this guy is The Player, even if he does have information known only to him."

"Are they aware of the information about Delia's ring?"

"Only Brandon. We're keeping that close to the vest, so maybe that's why."

They rode in silence for several seconds, each lost in their own thoughts until Jake broke it.

"The last time we talked on the phone, you already knew you were going to traipse off to meet Mitchell, didn't you?"

"I didn't know for sure it would work out, but that was my plan. Why?"

He traced his finger around the curve of her ear and she shivered. "You told me you loved me. Did you say that because you thought it might be the last time we talked?"

"I said it because it's true." She closed her eyes. "The circumstances made it easier to say. Before, I didn't feel as if I had a right to declare my feelings while Fiona hated me and your ex didn't trust me."

"Neither of those things is the case anymore." He kissed his thumb and dragged it down the side of her throat. "I love you, too. When I thought I had lost you to Copycat Three, I felt dead inside."

Her throat closed and tears pricked the back of her eyes. "You've killed twice now to save me. You don't even have to tell me you love me. I'll take actions, any day."

"And I'll do it again, if necessary, but there are easier ways to show my love for you."

Several minutes later, they pulled into the public parking lot across from the Venice Canals and the walk streets that meandered through them. As they walked over the bridge to Quinn's house, clasped hands swinging, Kyra said, "Let's not talk too much about The Player tonight. Fill him in on the case, because he'll demand it, and then let's go easy. He's really upset at the thought of The Player still among the living."

"That's a deal. I'm burned out, myself."

They reached Quinn's red door, and Kyra knocked and called out at the same time, "We're here."

She cocked her head, listening for Quinn's response or footfall. On his better days, he answered the door himself. On other days, he invited her in and she used her key. Only silence answered this time.

"Quinn?" She dragged her keys from her purse and shoved the one to his house in the lock. She clicked open the door and hit it with her hip. "Quinn?"

She stepped inside with Jake close on her heels. Then she saw an arm splayed on the floor and a shock of silver hair. She charged forward and dropped to her knees beside Quinn's body.

"Quinn? Quinn?" She put her fingers at his throat, avoiding his blue eyes that had lost all their spark.

As Jake crouched beside her, she grabbed his arm. "He's dead, Jake. Quinn's dead."

* * * * *

Look for the final installment of Carol Ericson's
A Jake and Kyra Investigation series when
The Trap *goes on sale in July 2021!*

And don't miss the previous books in the series:

The Setup
The Decoy

Available now wherever Harlequin Intrigue
books are sold!

SPECIAL EXCERPT FROM

⊕HARLEQUIN

INTRIGUE

*Police handler Tate Emory is thankful that
Sabrina Jones saved his trusty K-9 companion, Sitka,
but he didn't sign up for national media exposure.
Exposure that unveils his true identity to the dirty
Boston cops he took down…and brings Sabrina's
murderous stalker even closer to his target…*

*Read on for a sneak preview of
K-9 Hideout by Elizabeth Heiter.*

Desparre, Alaska, was so far off the grid, it wasn't even
listed on most maps. But after two years of running and
hiding, Sabrina Jones felt safe again.

She didn't know quite when it had happened, but
slowly the ever-present anxiety in her chest had eased.
The need to relentlessly scan her surroundings every
morning when she woke, every time she left the house,
had faded, too. She didn't remember exactly when the
nightmares had stopped, but it had been over a month
since she'd jerked upright in the middle of the night,
sweating and certain someone was about to kill her like
they'd killed Dylan.

Sabrina walked to the back of the tiny cabin she'd
rented six months ago, one more hiding place in a series
of endless, out-of-the-way spots. Except this one felt
different.

Opening the sliding-glass door, she stepped outside onto the raised deck and immediately shivered. Even in July, Desparre rarely reached above seventy degrees. In the mornings, it was closer to fifty. But it didn't matter. Not when she could stand here and listen to the birds chirping in the distance and breathe in the crisp, fresh air so different from the exhaust-filled city air she'd inhaled most of her life.

The thick woods behind her cabin seemed to stretch forever, and the isolation had given her the kind of peace none of the other small towns she'd found over the years could match. No one lived within a mile of her in any direction. The unpaved driveway leading up to the cabin was long, the cabin itself well hidden in the woods unless you knew it was there. It was several miles from downtown, and she heard cars passing by periodically, but she rarely saw them.

Here, finally, it felt like she was really alone, no possibility of anyone watching her from a distance, plotting and planning.

Don't miss
K-9 Hideout *by Elizabeth Heiter,*
available July 2021 wherever
Harlequin Intrigue books and ebooks are sold.

Harlequin.com

HIEXP0621

Don't miss the first book in the new and exciting Last Ride, Texas series from _USA TODAY_ bestselling author

DELORES FOSSEN

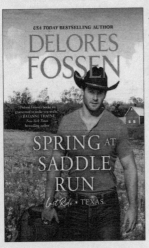

The residents of Last Ride, Texas, which is famous— or more accurately, _infamous_—for its colorful history, have no idea what's about to happen when the terms of Hezzie Parkman's will upend their small-town world...and they discover it's possible to play matchmaker from beyond the grave!

"Clear off space on your keeper shelf, Fossen has arrived."
—Lori Wilde, _New York Times_ bestselling author

Order your copy today!

HQNBooks.com

PHDFBPA0721

Love Harlequin romance?

DISCOVER.

Be the first to find out about promotions,
news and exclusive content!

Facebook.com/HarlequinBooks

Twitter.com/HarlequinBooks

Instagram.com/HarlequinBooks

Pinterest.com/HarlequinBooks

ReaderService.com

EXPLORE.

Sign up for the Harlequin e-newsletter and
download a free book from any series at
TryHarlequin.com

CONNECT.

Join our Harlequin community to
share your thoughts and connect
with other romance readers!
Facebook.com/groups/HarlequinConnection